THI

CW00801997

Margaret Brazear

Copyright © Margaret Brazear 2014

http://historical-fiction-on-
kindle.blogspot.co.uk

CHAPTER ONE

"What are you doing?"

Lord Morton stopped on the threshold of the large sitting room when he found his mistress seated beside the window, where she was admiring the embroidery cleverly crafted by his daughter. She looked up and greeted him with a dazzling smile but the smile froze on her lips when she saw his expression; he was angry and it showed. She had no right to be here, he had never wanted her here and now to arrive without invitation or warning and start talking to Madeleine as though she belonged...His Lordship was furious.

"Just talking to the child," she replied with a hesitant tilt of her lips, the beginning of a grin which he did not return. She had positioned herself, deliberately he thought, so that the sunlight caught her blonde curls and made them glow. "I had no idea there were children in the house," she went on.

The little girl looked at him with a smile of pleasure.

"Hello father," she said.

Olivia arched an eyebrow, and directed a look of surprise at Lord Morton.

"Madeleine," he replied. His face lit up with a delighted expression for the child but he made no move to approach. "What have you got there?"

Madeleine got to her feet and ran to him, holding out a finely embroidered scene on white silk. It was the view from the ground floor balcony of his Cornish house, copied from the painting which hung in her bedchamber. He held it up to better appreciate it and his heart skipped a beat. His daughter was very accomplished. She had captured the scene perfectly with her silks; the waves crashing against the shore were so lifelike he could almost hear them, could almost smell the salt sea air. She had even cleverly copied the footprints her mother had crafted in the sand when she painted the picture. He felt a note of pride mingled with sorrow and swallowed.

"Is that the screen cover for your mother?"

"Yes. I was finishing it in the garden, beside the lake, and this lady kindly expressed an interest. She was very complimentary about it."

He turned an angry frown on Olivia, who blushed and looked quickly away, then his expression softened as he looked back at the screen cover.

"So she should be," he said. "It is beautiful. But if it is finished you had best get it packed up and ready to send. We have time to catch the afternoon coach."

Madeleine folded the cover carefully, taking her time so as not to damage the delicate stitchwork, and placed it carefully into the fabric bag she held, another accomplishment of her needle.

"Yes father," she answered. "I have written a poem for her as well."

"What about?" He asked with a frown.

"It is only about Puddle."

Madeleine looked hopefully at her father and had begun to search in her bag for the poem, when Olivia asked:

"Who or what is Puddle?"

Richard scowled at her; he did not want her on friendly terms with his daughter and he very much wanted her to leave, but he had no wish to cause any unpleasantness in front of Madeleine.

"He is my dog," Madeleine replied breathlessly. "We called him puddle because when he was little he left puddles all over the place. Is that not right, Father?" He nodded and gave her an indulgent smile. "Can I send it with the screen cover?"

She spoke rapidly and joined all the words together, as though she had to get them all said before she forgot what she wanted to say or before somebody stopped her.

"You had best let me read it first," he said.

Madeleine took the parchment from her bag and passed it to her father, waited patiently while he quickly cast his eyes over it, smiling at the little dogs she had attempted to paint in the corners. Animals were never easy to draw and Madeleine's talent did not run in that direction, unlike her mother who was an accomplished artist. It did not matter; Philippa would be delighted with it whatever it looked like. Finally he nodded and smiled.

"It is delightful," he said giving it back to her. "She will love it. I'll wager she will put it in a little frame and hang it on her wall." He paused and waited expectantly for a few moments. "Anything else?" He asked. "No letter?"

Madeleine reluctantly produced an unsealed letter from her bag and passed it to her father. He had always read every letter she wrote to her mother but of late he had been obliged to remind her. He thought it likely that as his daughter was growing up, she felt it an imposition for him to approve her letters, or she might have something to say that she had no wish for him to read. Whatever it was, he did not like it.

His eyes narrowed as he read her neat handwriting. It told of her life here in London, of her exploits out and about with her dog and about the small academy he had found for her to attend; all harmless news until he reached the end.

"What is this?" He asked. He held out the letter and pointed to the last line where she had written: *Father misses you.* He arched an eyebrow.

She took the letter from him and rolled it up.

"I will change it, but it is true," she said stubbornly. "You do miss her. Do you think I do not notice you gazing at her portrait in my chamber?"

He had no answer for that. She was right, he had been unable to resist studying his wife's portrait whenever he was in his daughter's bedchamber. Indeed, he would feel much better if it did not hang there, then he would not be tempted, but that would be unfair to Madeleine and she would likely be angry with him if he took it down.

He would have to be more careful. Madeleine was no longer a child and her instincts were developing along with her body. She had begun to notice things and soon she would voice the questions which were in her mind. He would have to consider carefully what his answers would be. She had a right to an explanation, but she must never know the truth.

Gently, he put his arm around her shoulders and led her to the other end of the room, to the window which overlooked the courtyard and where Olivia could not hear. He glanced at the woman quickly to be sure she had not moved and lowered his voice as he spoke.

"You have to be very careful, before you express your own feelings, to be sure those feelings do not hurt someone else," he explained patiently. "If you tell her that I miss her, she might think there can be a reconciliation between us and that is simply never going to happen. Far better that she does not know. Do you understand?"

He told her the truth, but not the whole truth. His other reason for wanting that last line removed was because his own pride would not allow it. He never wanted her to know how much he missed her.

However she was living now, she had no need to know that. Madeleine nodded reluctantly.

"If you would only allow her to write back," she muttered, "you might discover that she misses you too."

Madeleine was indeed becoming her own person. She had never spoken to him quite so frankly before and he was unsure how to deal with this new, adult young woman.

He had made it a condition of allowing Madeleine to write to her mother and send gifts, that she did not write back. He was afraid of the things she might tell her and he was afraid of knowing what she was doing, who she spent her time with. She sent gifts, but nothing else.

He shook his head impatiently. He was trying very hard not to be angry but his daughter was growing up, of marriageable age according to the law, and it was only natural she wanted to know why her parents lived apart. He never wanted her to know the reason they parted or why they could never be reconciled. The truth might diminish her mother in her eyes and he did not want that.

"Madeleine, some things must be kept private and I refuse to discuss them, with you or anyone else." He squeezed her shoulder tighter and kissed the top of her head. "Now go and cut off that last line, then pack the things so we can despatch them on the next coach."

"I suppose you will want to see it to be sure," she said with an obstinate pout which made him laugh.

"Do I need to?" He replied. "Or can I trust you?"

Madeleine nodded and ran from the room, clutching the bag containing the precious gifts for the mother she never saw, while he watched her go, feeling unsettled by their conversation. Once certain she was out of earshot, he turned an angry scowl on Olivia who still sat beside the window, her green velvet gown spread out around her, her blonde hair curled on top of her head, her perfume permeating the air and overpowering the scent of flowers from the various vases about the room. His eyes swept over her with distaste.

"What are you doing here, My Lady?" He demanded. "I did not invite you."

"I was riding close by and I thought to surprise you," she answered nervously. "We never spend time in your house, only in mine."

"There is a reason for that."

He could see he was making her uncomfortable, but he could not care much. She should not have come here, she had no right. He saw her attempts to dismiss his mood, but he would not help her.

"You did not tell me you had children, My Lord," she remarked. "If you had I would have understood why you did not want her to see us together."

"Madeleine is private. I talk about her to no one." Still he made no move to approach her and she began to look even less comfortable. "I did tell you I was married."

Lord Morton scrutinised his mistress, knowing that by coming to his house, by intruding into the home of his daughter, she had put an end to their relationship. He felt no particular sadness about that, only the inconvenience of having to replace her.

"You did not tell me you still had contact with your wife," Olivia said. "You gave me the impression you had no contact with her at all, that your marriage was over."

"The marriage is over. I have had nothing to do with her since I left my house in Cornwall seven years ago. Not that you need to know that."

She still looked uncomfortable and was trying desperately to lighten the mood, that was apparent. Lord Morton could see she was regretting her invasion of his home, but it was too late now. One aristocratic whore was easy enough to replace with another.

"Yet you allow the child to write, to send her gifts," she went on with a disapproving frown.

He did not feel the need to justify his decisions to her or anyone else, but he had the strong suspicion that if he refused to answer her questions, she would never give them up. All he wanted from her now was her absence, from his house and his life.

"She is her mother," he said at last. "She has not seen her since she was five years old, but she was a good mother, if a poor wife. Madeleine must never believe she was abandoned by her mother."

Olivia studied the scowl on his handsome face for a few minutes before she spoke again.

"You have never told me why you live apart," she went on.

"It is not your affair. I will not discuss her; it would be unfair to Madeleine."

It would also be too hard for him, too painful, although he would never admit that to anyone, especially not to this woman for whom he had little, if any respect. Olivia stared at him warily, her eyes filled with doubt.

"Was she an adulteress?" She asked at last in a sympathetic tone.

His eyes met hers but he said nothing for a few moments. He did not want to answer that question for many reasons, not least of which that he did not trust her to keep the knowledge to herself. He wanted no one to know how his wife betrayed him, not to salve his own vanity but because one day his daughter might get to hear of it and that he never wanted.

"That is not your business, Madam," he replied at last.

Olivia got to her feet and walked quickly toward him. She stood before him and gripped his folded arms with her long, elegant fingers and her expression was one of compassion.

"Your refusal to condemn her speaks to your goodness," she murmured. "How awful for you, my dear."

She had apparently decided to take his refusal to answer as an affirmative.

He made no attempt to unfold his arms, to touch her. He was still angry; he wanted nothing of his life outside the house to touch Madeleine and Olivia had broken that rule, albeit a rule she had no knowledge of. He had avoided telling her where he lived, he had even told her it was private. She must have made enquiries to learn the whereabouts of his house, enquiries which would draw attention to him and to his daughter.

"If my wife is an adulteress, My Lady," he asked harshly, "then what are you?"

She released her grip and took a step back.

"I beg your pardon?"

"Are you not an adulteress as well?"

She gave a fleeting smile.

"I am a widow, My Lord," she argued. "I am no longer married."

"But I am and you know I am. That state does not prevent you from sharing my bed. I believe that makes you no better than my wife."

"Richard!" She gasped. "That is a terrible thing to say to me. What are you trying to do to our relationship?"

"We have no relationship, Madam," he answered coldly. "You have come here, uninvited, against my wishes, and intruded on my private life. You have had the audacity to introduce yourself to my daughter. I trust you were not asking her inappropriate questions about her mother."

"Inappropriate?"

"Of the kind you have been asking me. My wife is none of your concern, my life is none of your concern. I am sorry if that is not what you wish to hear, but I would be thankful if you would leave now and not return. I wish never to see you again."

Olivia merely stood and stared at him, her cheeks flushed and her eyes round and frightened.

"I am sorry, Richard," she murmured. "You are right; I should not have come here without your permission. It will not happen again."

"No, it will not." He still stared at her threateningly for a moment. "I will thank you to keep to yourself what you have learned this day. If you do not, you will regret it. I am quite sure there are things about you that you would not want the world to know."

She was silent for a little while, then she turned her back on him and went to look through the window at the garden outside. For a London house, it had a lot of ground and the gardens were beautiful, full of lovely flowers and shrubs. She saw a ball in the air followed by a dog chasing after it, Madeleine chasing after him. It was quite a big dog, long haired and a beautiful golden colour, and Olivia imagined it would be very smelly when it got wet, as it was doing now, chasing the ball into the lake. Madeleine laughed and Olivia smiled at the scene. She turned back to look at Richard but found him still in the same place, still with his arms folded, still showing his anger.

"Can you come for supper tonight, My Lord?" She asked. She moved toward him and let her fingers trail along his arm as she murmured seductively: "I can make it up to you."

He stood rigidly, made no attempt to respond to her advances in any way. She had been a good mistress, but he had lost all interest in her now and all he wanted was for her to remove herself from his presence.

He only stared at her coldly.

"I thought I made my position clear, My Lady. You and I are no more. I will not have my privacy invaded. Leave, please, before Madeleine returns and finds you still here."

"But Richard," she protested. "You cannot mean that. I love you."

He frowned and glared at her with a clenched jaw.

"I doubt that," he said. "But in any event, I do not love you."

"I thought..........."

"You thought wrong. Please leave."

At that moment he heard his daughter returning and he turned and left the room in order to forestall her.

"Come, Madeleine," he said, catching her hand as she approached. "You need to go to the kitchen and dry that dog, give him a good brush before he comes in the house."

She smiled happily, and handed him the parcel containing her gifts.

"You will take them to the coach?" She asked.

"I will." He took the parcel and released her hand. "Now go, before Puddle stinks the house out."

Once more he watched her go, feeling the affection of a proud father. Seeing her beside Olivia had unsettled him, made him realise that she was fast becoming a woman. He could see tiny buds which promised full breasts in the not too distant future and her figure was slowly forming, her waist narrowing ever so slightly, her hips beginning to flare. He needed to find a responsible female companion who could instruct her in the ways of life, not the nurse or maids she had now. She needed to know how a woman's body worked and he did not feel qualified to teach those lessons himself.

He sighed heavily, wishing with all his heart that the teacher could be her own mother. He made his way to Madeleine's bedchamber where hung the landscape in oils of the view from the back of his Cornish house, the original from which Madeleine had copied the embroidered screen cover she was sending. His wife had painted it, had sent it to decorate Madeleine's chamber shortly after they came to live in London. She was a very accomplished artist and had even sold some of her work privately. Richard had always been proud of her talent and he felt that glow of pride even now as he stared at the painting.

He recalled every word of the letter which had accompanied it, a letter addressed to him, begging that Madeleine be allowed to hang it, to remind her of her home.

His throat ached when he recalled those words, *her home.* London would never be her home, not really, not when as a small child she so loved to run along the beach, to take off her shoes and stockings and play in the waves. He caught back a sob as his memory showed him the pair of them, Madeleine and her mother, running back to where he stood laughing on the balcony, with their skirts soaked and waving their shoes and stockings in the air. The wind would catch their hair and pull it away from their flushed faces and he sharply recalled the joy he felt at the sight; he well remembered his daughter's disappointment to find there were no huge, crashing waves in London, no proper sand. The mud banks of the Thames simply would not do.

That is when he bought her the puppy, a companion to play with in the vast grounds of the London house, and what a wonderful companion he had turned out to be. Madeleine adored that dog and Richard had to admit he had sneaked his wet snout into his heart as well. He had a sudden vision of Philippa with the dog, although they had never met, and he knew that she too, would love him. She loved animals, all sorts of animals. He imagined her running through the waves with Madeleine and Puddle, how she would laugh. He could almost see her beautiful smile and her wave to him as they ran up the beach to the house. The memories brought tears to his eyes and he wiped them away with his fingers.

He missed his house, he missed walking along the beach with his daughter and his wife. He began to toy with the idea that it might be possible for Madeleine to learn those essential lessons from her mother, from the one person who should give them. But she would have to come here to London; he could not allow Madeleine to go there, not the way things were; that was something he would never consider. But would her mother leave Cornwall? He had no idea but it was a notion to ponder.

As one of the King's courtiers he had been called upon to help find a valid motive for him to dissolve his marriage to Queen Catherine and it occurred to Richard that he could have dissolved his marriage to Philippa without too much effort. Adultery was a crime as well as grounds for divorce, although such claims went on for years sometimes. But he had no desire to punish her or to be free of her and he would never marry again; that path led only to heartache.

Punishing his wife for her adultery would not ease the pain he had carried with him for seven years; revenge was not what he wanted either. The only thing that would make him happy would be the ability to go back to a time before it happened, when she still loved him. But that was impossible, so dwelling on it was a futile exercise.

Hanging on Madeleine's wall, beside the picture of the beach, was a small portrait of his wife, as she had looked the day he went off to fight the King's war. Just looking at her made him angry and he was never sure if it was because of her betrayal or because he still yearned for her, still loved her. Had he not been away for so long, it might never have happened, but the fact that it did would always haunt him.

He had a lot to think about and he was still pondering his ideas when he retired to bed for the night. He had grown used to sleeping alone, at least in this bed. None of the women he had taken to satisfy his needs had been allowed to visit this house, much less share this bed, the bed which still held the memory of Philippa. He was still angry with Olivia for having the effrontery to think she could come here, to the home he kept pure and sacred for his daughter.

As he had told her, Philippa was a good mother, if a poor wife. She would be the ideal person to teach Madeleine what she needed to know but although he had always tried to put his daughter first in all things, he realised he could not bring himself to contemplate seeing his wife again. Just thinking about her made him angry and hurt, even enraged him, so heaven alone knew if he could tolerate actually living under the same roof with her. He would not trust her alone with Madeleine. He was not really sure why, perhaps because she had been unfaithful to him and he was afraid she might corrupt Madeleine's innocence with her immorality.

He had been away for a year, fighting alongside the King in his war against France, and had trusted his brother to run his estate and care for his wife. Perhaps Stephen had misunderstood what he meant when he asked him to care for his wife, perhaps he thought he meant more than to be sure of her safety. Had he the slightest suspicion that Stephen could not be trusted to keep his hands off his brother's wife, he would never have left her alone with him, much less extracted his promise to keep her safe. If that was his idea of keeping her safe, it certainly was not Richard's.

All he could really remember now was his blind rage when he returned from that war, when he made the long journey to Cornwall by coach, feeling happy and excited at the prospect of seeing his wife, anticipating the warmth of her arms, the touch of her flesh against his, only to find her with child.

He had ordered Madeleine's things packed, he had ordered his own things packed and he had left. Despite Philippa's attempts to plead with him, he brought his little girl to London and never saw her or his brother again.

He shook his head in an attempt to banish the image his thoughts had dragged up from the past, where he desperately tried to keep it buried. No, he did not believe he could face her again. Seven long years had done nothing to ease his pain, nothing to dispel his fury. He thought it likely he would kill her if he met with her, as he almost killed her then, as he would have killed her had she not escaped him.

There was but one thing which stopped him going after her and that was Madeleine's pale little face at the nursery window, her pale and frightened little face which looked down at him from her bedchamber on the nursery floor where she had hidden away from the unfamiliar shouting and weeping.

He still dreamed about that day, still woke in the night angry enough to kill, his fists clenched, his heart broken and he wondered why he deserved the torture of reliving the whole, horrible scene over and over again. He would have given almost anything for one night when he was not revisited by the misery of that time.

His manservant woke him early the following morning and he was grateful to be roused from dreams of that day, from the murderous thoughts which had followed him into sleep.

Thomas had been with him for many years, but had always served in the London house so he knew nothing about the quarrel, only that His Lordship no longer lived with his wife, no longer visited his estate in Cornwall or wrote to his brother.

"I have an urgent message from your brother, My Lord," the servant told him.

Richard frowned angrily. It was something of a coincidence that he should be greeted with this after a night of dreaming about the man, of dreaming about him sharing his wife's bed, in her arms, sharing with her that which only her husband should share.

"What does he want?" He demanded.

"It is from the Monastery of Blackfriars," said the servant. "I regret to inform you that your brother is dying, My Lord. He is asking for you."

The idea that Stephen might be dying actually filled him with pleasure and he was unsure how to cope with that emotion. Whatever he had done, he was still his brother but Richard felt no sorrow for his anticipated passing. He would have been dead when Richard discovered his betrayal had he not escaped into the fields surrounding the house, had he not hidden away while Richard was desperately trying to comfort a terrified five year old whose world had exploded into screams and sobs.

He would have killed him then and felt no sorrow, so why should he feel sorrow now. The man deserved nothing, certainly not a visit from the older brother he betrayed.

His next thought was that if Stephen was dying, and dying in a London monastery at that, Philippa was alone. He was not certain how he felt about that, if he would use the knowledge to visit or write, but to what end? He could never forgive her so why torment himself further?

"What is he dying from? Something painful, I hope."

The servant drew a deep breath of disapproval. He knew about the rift between the two brothers, although he knew nothing of the details, but he thought it very bad form to deny someone their dying wish, especially a brother.

"I was only told that he was stabbed and the wound was left untreated, My Lord."

Richard knew it was unlikely his brother was stabbed in a fair fight, knowing his character as he did and he was curious, but not curious enough to want to see him. He remembered his feelings last night about his wife, how he was sure he would kill her if ever she appeared before him, and he felt no different about his brother. The fact that he was already dying and likely bedridden, made no difference. He would still want to kill him and he had no desire to drag up those emotions again, but he might have to satisfy his curiosity.

All these years Richard had assumed Stephen was living in his house, continuing his relationship with his wife. He had not bothered to learn otherwise, just made sure neither of them received any funds from him. She was having his child so it seemed logical they would be together once he had gone and taken Madeleine away from the corruption in the house. So what was he doing in London, living out his final days in a monastery? Perhaps they had not been content in their treacherous relationship after all, or perhaps he thought he would more easily earn forgiveness for his sin in a religious establishment.

He wondered what on earth he could possibly have to say to the man. Should he reminisce about their childhood, share fond memories of their parents, their youth? He only had one memory to share with Stephen and that was not one he ever wanted to share with anyone. Yes, he would definitely feel that murderous fury if he ever laid eyes on him again; indeed he could feel it now, just talking about him.

"I have no interest in seeing him," he said at last. "If he has anything to say to me, he can write it down."

"He is dying, My Lord," the servant persisted. "Forgive my impertinence, but will you not regret it if you ignore him, if you deny him his last wish?"

"No, Thomas," Richard replied, "I will not forgive your impertinence, any more than I will forgive my brother's betrayal."

Thomas waited a few moments to see if His Lordship would have more to say, to see if he would change his mind.

"Very well, My Lord," he replied reluctantly. "Will you come down for your breakfast?"

Richard shook his head then wondered how his brother had got this injury. The speed with which he had taken himself off that day declared his cowardice. He had bedded his brother's wife, left her with child, but did not have the courage to stay and defend her. Richard was rather pleased about that, when he had time to stop and think. At least she would know the manner of man for whom she had thrown away a good marriage.

But he was intrigued. If he knew the name of the man who had stabbed Stephen, he could seek him out and thank him.

Thomas had a hand on the door knob and was about to leave the chamber when his master stopped him with a question.

"Who stabbed him?" He asked.

Thomas stood still and turned back to look at him, hopeful that His Lordship might have changed his mind about visiting his dying brother.

"A woman, I believe, My Lord," he replied. "A serving girl from the local tavern. She is in Newgate awaiting trial, though I am unsure when that will be. I heard they are waiting for the outcome, waiting to see whether to charge her with murder or unlawful wounding. Have no fear; she will be punished."

Richard was even more intrigued by this information. He could think of few reasons why a woman would stab a man she did not know, especially a nobleman. Either she was trying to rob him and a struggle ensued, or he did something to her to which she objected. Or perhaps she did know him; perhaps he had been living with her and there was an argument. It seemed unlikely; Stephen was always conscious of his elevated position in life, but then he had not seen him for eight years and he had no idea how he had been living. Richard cut off all financial assistance when he discovered his betrayal, so there was no telling what he had come to. Suddenly, from not caring either way, he felt he had to know.

"Do we know why she stabbed him?"

Thomas shook his head but continued to look at his master, until he was dismissed by a nod of His Lordship's head. Of course nobody knew why the woman had stabbed his brother; nobody would have bothered to ask. He was a viscount, she a mere serving girl and one from a tavern at that. Nobody would care why she stabbed him, only that he was dying and someone had to pay.

Richard thought the most likely explanation was that the woman was a pickpocket, that Stephen had tried to hold on to his purse and had been stabbed in the struggle. But something was telling him he needed to learn more, if only for his own peace of mind.

The door opened and Thomas returned, carrying bread and ale.

"I will go," Richard said reluctantly, "I want to hear what he has to say."

The monk he followed through the dark and cold stone corridors of the monastery was ancient. He seemed to Richard to be almost as old as the building itself and he had difficulty in walking, dragging one foot along behind him as though it were too heavy to lift. Richard was anxious to get this over and wanted to hurry the man, but he knew it would do no good. He was obviously incapable of walking any faster.

At last he stopped before an arched door and turned mournful eyes on Richard.

"Your brother is in here, My Lord," the monk said in a very quiet voice, as though afraid of waking the occupant, or waking the ghosts of this dismal place. "He is very weak. He has had Last Rites; you should prepare yourself. I think it unlikely he will be with us much longer."

Richard was growing impatient and wanted to shake the man or push him out of the way so he could get this done. The knowledge that he was about to face the one man in the world he wanted to murder did nothing to calm his mood.

"Then you had best hurry, Brother," he said. "There is little time to stand and gossip."

The monk drew himself up as much as possible in his crooked body and pushed open the door. Inside was a narrow bed beside a small table, a barred window and a crucifix on the wall above the head of the man who lie sleeping. Richard stepped inside and turned to be sure the monk had left them. He wanted no witnesses, just in case he felt an irresistible urge to hold the pillow over his brother's face.

He leaned over and looked at him. He had not changed much, still had the same unlined face, still the same trimmed beard although there was a little grey at his temples. He had lost a lot of weight, and Richard felt pleased about that. His refusal to subsidise his limited income had paid off; the man had struggled. Good – it was what he deserved. He was not so comfortable with the idea that Philippa, too had struggled. He did not understand why he should feel any more sympathy for her plight; she deserved no better than Stephen.

His brother's breathing was ragged but Richard could only stare at him, hoping he would die there and then and spare him the need to talk to him. He was toying with the idea of turning round and going home when Stephen's eyes opened slowly and he gave a weak smile of satisfaction.

"You came," he murmured.

"Obviously," Richard said.

"Richard, thank you so much for coming," Stephen said.

He struggled in vain to sit up but his brother made no attempt to assist him.

"What do you want?" Richard demanded.

"Did they tell you I am dying?" Stephen spoke in a self pitying tone, as though expecting sympathy and affection from his only brother. He would be disappointed. All Richard felt was a need to hurry him along, to tell him to die now if he was going to and leave him to continue with the lonely life to which he had condemned him.

He waited for a reply, but when none was forthcoming he went on in a painful whisper.

"I do not want to leave this life estranged from my only brother," Stephen explained. "I need your forgiveness."

"That you will never have," Richard answered coldly.

He took a step back, away from the bed. Much as he tried to fight it, his memory was full of that day, of how this man had made him feel, and he wanted to take his throat between his strong hands and squeeze out what little life was left. He was not sure he could control himself if he had to stay in this room much longer. His fists clenched and his jaw shuddered as he ground his teeth together, wanting to lash out with those fists to relieve his anger. Even after seven years he felt almost as angry today as he had then.

"Please, Richard," Stephen begged. "Take my hand. I do not have long and if you forgive me, my time in purgatory will be shortened."

Richard did not want his time in purgatory shortened; if he had the power, he would lengthen it.

"You do not want me to come closer, Stephen, believe me. That would not be a good idea at all."

"What can I do to make it up to you? I am so very sorry."

"If that were true, you would have sought forgiveness years ago, not waited until now when you are afraid of what lies beyond. Just as then, you are a coward. I disowned you as my brother that day and I see no reason to change my mind now." He paused thoughtfully for a few minutes, wondering again about the woman awaiting trial in Newgate. "Why did this woman stab you?"

"She had no reason. I only wanted to touch her; she should have complied."

Richard stared at him, stunned into silence, wondering if there could be another interpretation of his brother's words than the one he was hearing.

"You wanted to touch her?" He demanded. "And she was unwilling?"

"She said she was, but we all know what that means."

"I know what it means, yes, but apparently you do not."

"They all say that to fire our passions. They do not mean it and when I did as she obviously wanted, she drew out a knife and stabbed me with it. Bitch!"

Lord Morton stared at his brother for a few moments, trying to gather his thoughts into a coherent interpretation of his words. A voice in the back of his mind was crying out, desperately trying to be heard: *He forced me, Richard! Please believe me!* He would not listen; he was too angry, his only wish was to get as far away from her as possible, to take Madeleine, protect her from the corruption in the house. He thought he knew his brother well, thought he knew that Philippa had to be lying, that Stephen would never take a woman by force. She had seduced him and now she was afraid and trying to lay the blame at his door.

And there was another voice, the voice of his old nurse who had raised him from birth. He had forgotten she was there, that she, too, had pleaded. *Wait, Richard! Tell me what has happened!* She had called to him as he strode away from the nursery, carrying Madeleine in his arms.

He began to shake his head, unbelievingly, trying to tell himself he had not been wrong; he could not have been wrong. Now his anger was growing again and he took another step away from the bed, using all his willpower to summon the courage to ask the question.

"Did my wife also tell you she was unwilling?"

Whatever the answer would be, he was very much afraid of it. Either reply would bring his world crashing about his ears, collapsing just as it had then.

Stephen drew a deep breath, a shuddering breath which was obviously painful, and at last looked ashamed.

"I thought she was teasing, like all the others. Richard, I saw the way she was with you. It was obvious she enjoyed being touched, so how was I to know? I thought she would be glad of the attention, with you being away for so long. Why should she refuse me?" His voice began to fade and he closed his eyes for a moment. He reached out a hand to the pitcher on the stand beside him. "Can you pass me some water, please?"

Richard made no move to help him, only stared in disbelief at this man who he had loved, who he had played with as a child, who he had grown to manhood beside.

"You asked me to look after her," Stephen said.

"I did not ask you to take my place in her bed!" Richard shouted. "What sort of depraved monster are you?"

"It was only once, Richard," Stephen replied. "That is all, just once. She locked me out of her chamber after that, so I realised that perhaps I had a made a mistake."

He could only stare at him, not sure whether he trusted himself to speak. He felt that if he tried to voice a single word he would burst into tears and he never wanted to break down before this man.

At last Stephen drew a deep breath and swallowed hard.

"After the row," he said, "when you had gone, I went home and Alice threw me out. Can you believe it? Of all people to turn against me, our nurse who was like a mother to us. She would not listen, said if I did not leave she would kill me herself."

Richard looked at him with disdain; he heard nothing of regret, no thought for Philippa, for Madeleine, for his brother - all he heard was self-pity.

"Were you ever going to tell me this? Why did you not write, tell me the truth?"

"I was afraid of what you would think of me."

"What I would think of you? What about what I thought of her? Did it never occur to you the damage you did? I thought she betrayed me, when all the time…you destroyed my marriage, you stole seven years of my life, of Philippa's life, you caused Madeleine to grow up without a mother. Am I hearing this right?"

"You were angry, I could see that the night you left. I was afraid; I thought you would kill me so I rode away."

Richard felt his knees growing weak and he desperately wanted to sink down onto the bed, but he would not trust himself that close to his brother. He wanted to kill him even more now. He had believed his wife was still living with him, still being unfaithful to her marriage vows. He had imagined the three of them, her, Stephen and their bastard child, living happily together in his house, and now he was telling him it was only once and she had locked him out. What had she suffered all this time, alone, unable to make him believe the truth?

He recalled one of her early letters, the one that came first though some weeks after he had left. She explained then what had happened, but he did not believe it. He had read it once then tossed it into the fire in contempt. How dare she accuse his brother of rape? He thought. But she was telling the truth and he had stolen all this time from her and from Madeleine, he deprived both his wife and himself of the love they had treasured since the day they wed. He felt sick.

"Richard," Stephen was whispering reaching out his hand, which his brother ignored. "You will forgive me?"

"For ruining my life and the life of the woman I love? Do you have any idea what I did to her while you were galloping away to safety? Do you care? No, I will not forgive you. I hope you burn in hell for all eternity."

"Richard, please, it was nothing. You did not have to make such a big thing out of it. I told her not to tell you; it was foolish of her."

Again he was stunned. Stephen did not even know that his depravity had born fruit. Oh, God! What a mess his life had become.

"You are not even sorry, are you?" Richard demanded. "You are only sorry you might go to hell for your crimes. You have no regrets for what you did, only that you got caught."

"Richard, I am sorry, I swear..."

"This woman who stabbed you, did you bother to learn her name?"

Stephen turned his head to look at his brother hopefully and there was a little smile on his lips.

"Sarah," He said hopefully, "Sarah Tenby. You are going to the prison to take revenge?"

"I am going to the prison to free her and give her my heartfelt thanks."

CHAPTER TWO

The smell hit him as he rode toward Newgate prison, when he could barely see the outline of the grim building. He had heard tales of the stench which permeated from the place, so bad that nearby shops were forced to close in summer as people could not function with it. His horse baulked as he got closer and he had to dismount and lead him to a nearby post, where a barefoot young boy, wearing a dirty rag to cover his nose and mouth, sat with a bucket of water watching another horse. Richard gave him a coin and walked across the road to the prison gates.

He asked for the woman and the guard looked up in surprise.

"Who are you?" He asked insolently.

"I am the Earl of Morton," Richard replied. "And I wish to see Mistress Tenby."

"Isn't it your brother she attacked?"

"It is. Why? Does that matter?"

At last the man got to his feet but his expression was doubtful, as though he found Richard's request unusual, and it probably was.

"Sorry, My Lord," he said, "but if you've come for some sort of revenge, I have to tell you I cannot allow that. Besides, she will be swinging from the end of a rope soon enough. You can come back and watch if you want."

What a ghastly idea!

"I want to see whoever is in charge if this gruesome place," he demanded. "I want to see him now."

The guard turned away and whispered to another guard who waited outside in the courtyard. The second guard walked off while Richard waited impatiently. He did not want time to remember the day his life ended, that day when he had been angry enough to murder both his wife and his brother, two people he had, until that moment, loved.

It seemed an interminable length of time before the guard eventually returned followed by an older man, who opened a small gate and beckoned him inside.

"I have come to free the woman named Sarah Tenby," Lord Morton said. "She acted in self defence."

"My Lord," the man said. "I do not understand. She stabbed your brother, and from what I understand the wound has not healed. He is dying. She is to hang."

"There cannot have been a trial yet, surely. What has become of the law in this country? She is entitled to a fair trial."

"Well, My Lord, there will be a trial, of course, but it is an obvious case of guilt. She stabbed him; we assume she was trying to steal from him and he struggled."

Strange, Richard assumed the same this morning, before he had spoken to his brother.

"Did you ask her why she stabbed him?"

"No, My Lord. It did not seem necessary."

"I will tell you why Mistress Tenby stabbed my brother, shall I?" He said angrily. "Because he tried to rape her, just as he has done before. He confessed it to me only half an hour since, and he is, as you say dying. Unlikely he would lie about a thing like that. I want her released, at once."

The man bowed his head and turned to the guard.

"Release the woman," he said. "I will go and draw up the necessary papers."

"I will wait here," Richard said.

He did not trust the warders of this place to do as they said and release her and he was going nowhere until he was sure. He could do little to make amends for his treatment of his wife, but at least he could be sure this poor woman was treated fairly.

While he waited, he tried to keep hold of his breath to avoid breathing in the stench of the place, but it was a hopeless task and he could only hope he would not have long to wait. Far worse than the sickening smell were the sickening memories that forced their way into his mind. He concentrated his thoughts on the dark and dismal buildings, on the barred windows, tried to give his intellect over to the crimes of the occupants behind those bars, but he was relieved when the warder returned, holding Sarah Tenby roughly by the arm.

She was a very pretty girl, no more than sixteen or so, with auburn hair and green eyes and it occurred to Richard that with a little money to clean herself up and buy some decent clothing, she might well be a beauty.

As the warder dragged her closer, he glared at him angrily.

"There is no need to be so rough," he said. "The woman is innocent."

The woman was also terrified. Her huge green eyes were wide and frightened and he noticed her lips trembling. He thought it likely she did not believe he had come to rescue her, but had other ideas. He could hardly blame her; the chasm between the law for the nobility and that for the lower classes was wide and grossly unjust.

He took her arm gently and led her outside and away from the prison. The stench spread a long way, too far to escape it with only a few steps, but he led her to where he had left his horse, far enough away so she need not fear she would be thrust back inside.

"Sarah," he said gently, passing her a velvet purse. "I want you to have this money. It is no compensation for what you have suffered, but it will help you on your way at least. I am deeply sorry for my brother's actions. Do not try to forgive him; he does not deserve it."

He mounted his horse and prepared to ride away, leaving her looking puzzled and saying nothing. At last she seemed to emerge from her trance and grabbed hold of his foot where it rested in the stirrup.

"Thank you, My Lord," she said. "Thank you so much. Now I can go home to Yorkshire, to my family who I should never have left. I hope they will forgive me."

He looked down at her with a kind smile.

"I am sure they will," he said. "We all make mistakes; all we can hope to do is learn from them." He reached down and lifted her hand to lips. "Take care now, Mistress. May God go with you."

The sand between Philippa's toes was warm and dry, covering her feet as they sank into the pale yellow softness. High up on the cliffs above rode two horsemen, and a man and his dog walked along by the water's edge. It was a beautiful day, the morning sun hot and only a slight breeze coming off the ocean.

She thought about how hot and sticky it would be in London, how the dust from many horses and carriages would stick to their clothing and make their hair dusty. Madeleine should be here, enjoying the beach as she had as a small child, not enduring the grime of the city.

She walked along the beach every morning and she often wondered why she wanted to torture herself. She could almost hear her little girl's laughter as she played her game of dodging the waves, running backwards before the water could touch her feet. Philippa could almost feel Richard's hand in hers, warm and comforting, making her feel secure, making her feel loved.

Without noticing it, she wandered closer to the ocean's edge and now she felt the cold spray on her face and shoulder as a wave splashed off a large rock.

Her little girl was twelve years old now, almost a woman. She wondered what sort of woman she was becoming, wondered if Richard had spoilt her too much to make up for the loss of her mother. But remembering her letters, the warmth and love which shone through each word, she knew she was growing into a nice woman, a woman who would one day insist on seeing her mother again.

That day would come, she knew it, and that day was the only thing she had left to look forward to; she just wished she knew when it would be, how long she would have to wait.

She came to the end of the beach which was part of the Morton estate and stopped for a moment, looking up at the cliff top, before she turned back. She had taken this walk every morning in all weathers. Sometimes she had worn her heavy fur lined cloak, her thick leather boots, some mornings she had been soaked through by the rain, but still she walked, her memories her only companions, and she never understood why.

Always she tried to banish Richard from her mind. She tried not to think about what he was doing or who he was with and she tried hard to convince herself that he did not believe his wife to be a whore, despite knowing that was precisely what he did believe. She tried not to remember his tender love, his friendship. Those memories hurt too much, so she filled her heart with anger and resentment to overpower them.

Sometimes when she returned to the house, she would pour herself some ale, sit at the table and write a letter to her husband, explaining once more that she was not to blame, that she did not seduce his brother, that she did not even like him. The first of these letters she sent off on the London coach, but there was never a reply. She wrote a few times more, once with the painting of the sea and twice about Madeleine. But these letters to Richard, declaring the truth, were never meant to be read, not by him. Still she wrote them, then she would take the letter to the kitchens and burn it to ashes in the stove. She had no more idea of why she wrote the letters than she did of why she took that beach walk every single day. It was a compulsion, something she had to do in order to function and she would not stop until she had her daughter back in her arms, until her husband took the time to listen.

As she approached the house she glanced up at the top floor and saw Alice's worried frown. She waved at the old nurse and forced a smile. She knew Alice watched her every morning, always afraid she might be tempted to drown her sorrow in the sea.

At home in his London house Richard watched Madeleine playing in the garden, throwing the ball for her dog, running after him and laughing as he chased it into the lake, no doubt frightening the fish and making himself smelly and impossible to clean.

He smiled at the sight, but his smile froze on his lips. He had kept this dear child away from her mother for seven years. He told himself it was the best thing, that his wife could easily corrupt their daughter with her immoral ways. He acted out of concern for Madeleine's wellbeing, so she would grow to be a good woman, uncorrupted and pure, ready to be faithful to whatever man had the honour to be her husband.

He had thought only yesterday she was almost a woman and now he knew she had grown to that stage without her mother's guidance because her father was too arrogant to listen, too angry to stop and think about what he was doing.

Memories came back in a rush, memories he had carefully shut out. Now he must face them, each little detail of that day. He had been away, in France, fighting for the King. He had not seen his wife and child for that entire year; he had made do with only a few letters and none of them gave a hint of the tragedy awaiting him at home.

He travelled across country to his home in Cornwall, longing to hold his wife in his arms, longing to feel her soft flesh against his. It had been such a long time and he missed her so much. Theirs had been a perfect match; their mutual love and respect gave them a friendship most married couples never achieved, their mutual desires and passions gave them joy most couples never found. He knew she would yearn for him as he yearned for her; he knew that her passion and desire would be more intense than ever before. He could not wait to get to her.

She had been out, he could tell by her rosy cheeks and her hair which adhered to her forehead, by the damp hem of her grey velvet cloak. She still wore her gloves and her heavy boots and those boots were to save her, if only she had known. He heard her gasp when he called her name from the doorway, and she turned and smiled at him, but it was an uncomfortable sort of smile, as though she was happy to see him, but unsure if he would be happy to see her. He was too impatient, too fired up with wanting her to stop and think about what that hesitance might mean, even assuming he had noticed it which he was not sure he had, not then. It was only afterwards he realised what she was trying to tell him with that look.

He strode toward her, his arms outstretched, and pulled her into them, held her tightly against him. He kissed her hungrily, and as his fingers sought the fastening of her cloak he felt it - a flutter, a familiar gentle bumping against him and it was coming from her.

He had felt that before, when she was growing Madeleine within her womb. He stepped back and looked down, put his hand on her stomach and once more the little flutter tickled his palm. She gazed at him but only now did he remember the relief in her eyes, as though she were glad to have her secret out in the open.

She was with child and it could not be his.

"Richard, I am sorry, your brother............."

She got no further.

He hit her, hard, with the back of his hand and she screamed as she fell to the floor, her head banging against the wall. Now he vividly recalled the stream of blood which began to flow down the side of that lovely face and soak into the collar of her gown beneath the cloak, turning the delicate white lace to bright red.

She held her hand to her injured cheek while the blood poured between her delicate fingers and he could only stare at her, horrified. He realised something else as he recalled that time, as he dragged up those painful memories: at that moment he was not seeing her, he was not seeing his beautiful wife who he loved so much, who could do no wrong in his eyes. He was seeing a woman he did not know, a whore who would give herself to his brother the minute his back was turned.

"Richard, it is not what you think. Please, give me a chance to..."

Now his cheeks burned with shame as he forced himself to remember what happened next. He had shut his mind to it, he told himself he had no memory of what happened, but his dreams would never let him uphold that lie, never let him forget. Her pleading voice shocked him out of his reverie and he grabbed her arms and pulled her to her feet, then his hand came down hard upon her face, slapping her with his palm this time, leaving an horrible red mark which turned to a purple bruise later on, after he had gone; he never saw the damage but now his imagination was showing it clearly. He held fast to her arm so she could not escape him, and hit her again, many times.

He supposed on some level he must have realised the blood had come from a wound made by his heavy, ruby ring, that the stone had cut into her face and must have hurt her badly, but that did not stop him from hitting her again. Had she not kicked out at him with those heavy leather boots, yanked herself away and fled in terror, he might have killed her, he might have beaten her to death in his blind rage.

He marched from the chamber and went in search of Stephen, but he was too late. He had gone, saddled his horse and ridden away. Richard's anger was all consuming, like a fire which would not be dampened, when he looked up and saw that little frightened face in the window and he had gone into the house and prepared to leave for good.

He had the horses harnessed to the carriage, he had their boxes loaded on board, his own and his daughter's, and he lifted Madeleine inside. As he stood beside the carriage to take a last, wistful look at the house he loved, he heard those words that had rushed back to him today, as he stood looking down at his dying brother: *He forced me, Richard! Please believe me!*

He looked up at the window of the bedchamber that had been theirs, his eyes met those of his wife. He must have seen the blood soaked cloth she held against her face, but somehow the image failed to penetrate, failed to register as anything unusual. He turned and climbed into the carriage to begin the long journey to London. He could hear his wife calling out to him as the horses pulled them along the drive and he turned to his daughter, saw the fear in her pretty brown eyes, saw the tears which hovered around her lashes, and he put his arm around her and pulled her close to him. He wanted to tell her not to fret, that all would be well, but he could not lie to her and he had no idea if all would ever be well again.

He left Madeleine playing with her dog and made his way to his bedchamber where he laid down on his bed and put his hands behind his head to stare at the ceiling. His feelings were in so much turmoil, he had no idea what he should do or indeed if he should do anything. Were it not for his daughter, he might simply write to Philippa with an apology and leave it like that, but he could not do that, could he?

His memory was showing him more than he wanted to see. He closed his eyes and she was in his arms, her soft breath against his neck, her soft breasts against his. She whispered his name, told him she loved him, wrapped her arms around him and her breathing came in heavy gasps as he buried himself inside her, as they rose together to such heights of passion, he thought he would explode from the pleasure. These past years he had been afraid to remember that, to recall those wonderful nights in her arms, for fear he would imagine her with Stephen, giving that same passion to him. She was a sensuous woman and if he thought at all, he thought it likely the year of abstinence had been too much for her and she had turned to Stephen to fulfil that need. What a fool he was!

He stood up and went to the window which looked down on the gardens. He made up his mind as he watched Madeleine sitting on the grass, her arms wrapped around her very wet dog. He could almost smell the creature from here, but they both looked so happy. There was only one thing to do and he must do it, painful though it would be.

He went downstairs and outside and walked toward her; she jumped to her feet when she saw him and he noticed her frock was soaking and trails of wet mud decorated the fabric from shoulder to knee. She was almost a woman, but he could never imagine her in voluminous skirts and heavy material, with fancy collars and delicate sleeves. Puddle raced toward him and he stepped back, out of the way; he did not want to have to change his clothes.

"Madeleine," he said. "Please go and get changed, clean that dog as best you can and ask Nurse to pack your clothes, all of them."

The child's eyes grew round as she stared at him.

"Why, Father?" She asked after a moment. "Where am I going?"

"I am taking you to your mother," he replied. "It is a very long journey and we will have to stay overnight somewhere, possibly two nights, depending on how much time we can make."

"See Mother?" Her eyes grew wider as she stared at him, as though she were afraid to speak lest she had misheard. "Really?"

Her wide eyed expression of sheer wonder almost broke his heart. A child's visit to her own mother should not be something so bizarre as to cause her disbelief.

What the hell had he done?

"Yes, really," he replied.

"Puddle too?"

He smiled indulgently. He had no idea how the animal would cope with such a long journey, but he could hardly ask Madeleine to leave him behind, not when his intention was that she should not return to London.

"Puddle, too," he answered. "You had best be sure he has a bowl and lots of water, as well as food for the journey."

Still she stood and stared at him, looking concerned.

"We are really going to see Mother?" She persisted and he could hear a little catch in her voice.

"We are, and not before time. Now hurry, please. I want to make a start before it gets too late."

The dog had to be lifted into the coach as the step was too high, and he was a big dog. They would have to stop for him to attend to his natural business a few times and each time it would be up to Richard and the coachman to lift him inside. It was worth it to see the sheer joy on his daughter's face and he wondered how she had kept her counsel all these years, how she had resisted the temptation to ask him questions about her mother.

He could only suppose she sensed it was not a subject he wanted to talk about and she had respected that. She was a remarkable child.

Now he felt her eyes on him and he knew she was longing to question him, to find out why after all the precautions he had taken to prevent her knowing too much, suddenly he was taking her to see her mother.

"Madeleine," he began hesitantly. "I am sure you are wondering why I have had this sudden change of heart. You are old enough now to understand a little, I think. At least I hope so."

She said nothing but her eyes never left his, as though she was trying to anticipate his words before he spoke them.

"The fact is, I am ashamed to say that seven years ago I made some terrible mistakes and I did the worst thing anyone could do to a woman." He watched her eyes grow even rounder and she looked angry. "I took her child away from her," he went on. "I thought I was doing my best for you, but I was wrong; I was very wrong. I hope you will forgive me one day."

Madeleine got down from her seat and climbed over the sleeping, damp dog who took up the entire floor of the carriage, and she went and sat beside her father. She put her arms round his neck and kissed his cheek, then laid her head on his shoulder. She said nothing.

It was a very long journey and they had several stops along the way. The taverns they stopped at were reluctant to allow the dog in the bedchamber, but Richard had always found that money spoke louder than words, and money and position together spoke loudest of all.

Madeleine had not been inside an inn since he had taken her to London when she was but five years old, and he hoped she retained no memory of that day. She certainly seemed completely captivated by her surroundings and the grubby and roughly dressed clientele, as well as the smell of ale.

There was a prostitute plying her trade at a table in the corner and Richard was anxious to get his daughter away before she started asking questions, but the woman was dressed for her profession and was easy enough to spot, even for a naive twelve year old. As the man sitting beside her shoved his hand into her bodice, Richard turned quickly to find his daughter staring at the couple intently.

He turned her away and asked the innkeeper to send food up to their room, and was relieved when Madeleine made no mention of the scene.

They could not make enough time to finish the journey with just one overnight stop, probably because of the time they lost stopping for the dog, and Richard was deep in thought all the way there. Part of him was longing to return his daughter to her rightful place, longing to see the joy on the face of his wife, but the other part was afraid to face her. She had always greeted him with love, even that last time which had ended so disastrously, but this time he expected her to greet him with hatred and contempt and that was something he had no experience of. He was very scared he was about to get his heart broken all over again, but this time he would know it was his own doing.

Strangely enough, now he knew she had not been with Stephen all these years, it had not once crossed his mind that there might possibly be another man in her life. He had, after all, abandoned her so who could blame her if she had found someone worthier of her love? Now he did think of it, he wondered how he would cope with that. She was not free to marry; she was still his wife. Knowing how wrong he had been, he could not now believe she would break her marriage vows; if only he had realised that years ago.

It was not right, he thought, that she remained alone while he had filled her place with a variety of different women, each one a poor substitute for Philippa.

Now he had forced himself to face his memories about the last time he had seen his wife, he could not get them out of his mind and he anticipated their meeting with dread. He was a proud man, and it was not easy for him to admit he had torn their lives apart, had made a horrendous mistake for which no forgiveness could ever be forthcoming. He did not expect it, so he would not ask for it. What he did expect was that Philippa would hate him as he had tried hard to hate her. He expected nothing else - he was making this journey for Madeleine and as a peace offering, if such a thing could ever be accepted.

He would stay a few days, long enough to recover from the journey and see that Madeleine and Puddle were settled. Philippa would not want him there; it was still his house, but it had ceased to be his home the day he had viciously beaten the woman he loved and stolen her child away from her.

Now that child was excitedly peering out at the passing scenery, a smile on her lovely face and her eyes sparkling with joy. She did not speak very much, asked no questions, just watched the unfamiliar fields and stone cottages which she had never seen in London. Her father wondered if she remembered this scenery from when she lived here, before he snatched her away and taken her to the city.

If there was one thing he dreaded more than facing his wife again it was having to tolerate the child she would have borne to his brother. It would be nearly seven years old now and he had no idea if it were a boy or a girl. He had not enquired. Now he knew she had spent these years alone, he wondered if she kept the child with her or fostered it out to avoid scandal. He now knew it was much more likely she would have fostered the child to avoid a reminder of his brother's depravity, of what she had suffered at his hands. He hoped so.

But he had taken her daughter away, so she might not have wanted to part with another child, and what would that mean for Madeleine? He could not bear for her to get to her mother and find she had a brother or sister she knew nothing about. Perhaps it was wrong to have made this journey so impulsively; perhaps he should have written first, waited for her acquiescence, warned her so that she could arrange whatever she needed to for her daughter's arrival. His own arrival was of no matter; he would sleep at the village inn or in the barn if necessary. Madeleine was the important one in all this, Madeleine and her mother.

It was late afternoon when the carriage at last came to a halt in the driveway. Madeleine turned to look at him, her face full of excitement, her smile so infectious he could not resist smiling back. Then he nodded and she flung open the carriage door. Puddle may have needed help getting into the coach, but he had no difficulty getting out.

Madeleine followed him to the ground and took off at a run, while her father climbed down and stood watching her go, quite amazed that she remembered the way so well. She too must have vivid memories of this place; he could only pray that her memories of that last day were not as vivid.

CHAPTER THREE

From her nursery on the top floor of the house, Alice heard carriage wheels below on the cobbles and got stiffly to her feet to look out of the window. There were few visitors to the house who would arrive in a carriage and if it was someone who would disturb Lady Philippa with bad news, Alice wanted to be sure she was there to comfort her. That dear lady had endured enough bad news in her life and Alice was not about to allow any more.

She made her way slowly to the window, her legs stiff from sitting, and peered down at the courtyard, but she caught her breath in surprise to see Lord Morton step down from the carriage and stand for a few moments gazing at the house.

The years had not changed him much. He had lost a little weight, but still looked healthy and wealthy enough in his fine velvet clothes, while his countess scrimped and saved and borrowed just to make do, while she patched up her gowns and turned her shifts to give them more life. His dark hair shone like satin in the sunlight and watching him, she remembered the little boy he had once been, the little boy who had climbed onto her lap while she read to him and rocked him to sleep. He was always more affectionate that way than his brother. While she read to Richard, Stephen would be playing with his bricks, deeply absorbed in building them up and knocking them down. Perhaps that was an early sign of his desire to destroy, as he had destroyed his brother's marriage.

Her mouth turned down bitterly. She was right then; it was more bad news. How dare he come back here after the way he had left things, after the state in which he had left his wife? She wanted to run down and hit him with something heavy, but her common sense told her he must have a very good reason for having come all this way. She had not seen Madeleine, but then she had been slow getting to the window and she had no idea if he had brought her or not. If not, then why was he here alone? Was he wanting to dissolve the marriage after all this time, perhaps wanting to drag her lady through the courts, make his accusations publicly? Alice would kill him first.

She had raised both Lord Morton and his brother from birth and she was heartbroken at the way both of them had treated Lady Philippa. She felt it must be something she did wrong in their upbringing that had ruined that gentle and beautiful young woman. She felt guilty and she would always care for her, not only because of her guilt, but because she loved her like a daughter, had done since the day she came here as Richard's bride, little more than a child and completed besotted with him.

Alice always thought it was just the first flush of something new, that it would wear off given time and familiarity, but she had been happy to be wrong. She had never seen a married couple so devoted to each other, until that awful day when the world had gone dark for that dear lady.

As she watched, Richard finally walked slowly toward the house, leaving Alice undecided as to whether she should go down and protect Lady Philippa, give her support, or whether she would be better leaving them to say what had to be said in private. After all, it had been a very long time. But she swore she would not allow him to hurt her again, no matter what it took.

She had not heard from either brother since that day, and she was not sorry about that. She expected His Lordship would come looking for her at some point and she doubted she could be civil to him; she still seethed when she remembered not only the day he left, but the weeks after when she had nursed his beautiful wife, his heartbroken and devastated wife, who only stopped sobbing when she finally cried herself to sleep. The weeks when she thought she would lose her, that she would not recover would always be with her. She was so weak; she had not only lost a lot of blood, she had lost the will to go on.

Alice had begged her to let her write to Richard, but she did not want that. She was afraid, she said; what would she do if he refused to come?

Alice still found it hard to believe how he had behaved and she would never forgive him.

She watched him go inside the house then settled in a chair beside the window, ready to see if he came out again. She opened the window just a little more to be sure of hearing any unpleasantness which might ensue. Her memory of that day was still too raw to forget.

Philippa sat in a wicker chair on the ground floor balcony looking out at the white foam coming off the waves and gathering on the wet sand. She had her easel in front of her, but the desire to paint had left her along with her husband and child. She always tried, every day she would take her easel and palette to a beautiful spot and try to copy it, but it never worked. It was the only love he had left her with yet she did not want it, and she had felt like this for seven years; she saw no sign of that changing in the near future.

She had always loved to paint but now her efforts raised memories of a pretty little girl who sat beside her and watched with wonder as the landscape before her duplicated itself, as if by magic, on to the canvas. She remembered Madeleine's attempts to paint and although she had little talent for the art, her mother was always full of praise and encouragement, always told her she would improve as she got older, even knowing she would not. Encouragement and praise were very important to a child, and Philippa could only hope her husband had remembered that in his rearing of their daughter.

As she watched the waves she held an unwrapped parcel which had arrived that morning from her daughter in London. It was the last painting she had ever done, only this one was painted in delicate embroidery, which was Madeleine's special talent. The poem made her smile, especially her attempts at painting the dog and she was reminded of Madeleine's attempts to paint like her mother. Oh, how she wished she could share her joy with the little girl, how she wished she could hold her in her arms again. She would have grown into a young woman almost; Richard had been lenient enough to send regular portraits of her and it was good of him to allow the gifts, especially knowing how he felt. He made the concession for his daughter and if there was one thing for which she was thankful it was that he loved her and would always care for her.

Philippa knew she had nothing to worry about as far as her daughter's safety was concerned. Thinking about her now, she felt sad again, just as she did every time she received one of these gifts, felt she was missing out on her child's life and through no fault of her own. She was a good mother and she had been a devoted wife, whether her husband would believe it or not.

If Richard was keeping his word and not allowing Madeleine to believe her mother had abandoned her, one day when she was old enough, she would seek her out and know how much she was loved. Richard might even allow her to see her married if it was Madeleine's wish. That notion brought with it another; Madeleine was twelve years old now, the daughter of an Earl. She supposed that Lord Morton would already be well involved in negotiations for her marriage and that thought distressed her terribly. Not only would she have missed her daughter's entire childhood, but her husband had not even seen fit to write her about a marriage, involve her in negotiations or even inform her of who her daughter was to marry. God! How he must hate her! And how very much in love they had once been; they believed that nothing in this life or the next could ever come between them.

She heard a noise and turned to see a beautiful dog racing toward her, obviously wanting to make friends. She stood and stroked his head, then looked out toward the beach, expecting to see someone in search of the dog. It was a private beach, part of the Morton estate, but Richard never minded people walking their dogs there. Yet she could see no one and the dog did not look as though he had come from the beach. There was no sand on his paws and he was dry, but she had never seen him before and hoped he was not lost. Or perhaps she hoped he was lost; then she could keep him. She smiled to herself at the idea. If she wanted a dog, why not get one? Why wait for a stray to come along?

When she heard footsteps running towards the balcony from the house, running fast, Philippa thought she had found the dog's owner. The footsteps sounded like those of a child and being curious, she turned. She collapsed back into her chair, her breath almost stopping in her lungs.

She was taller than her mother had imagined she would be, almost as tall as her, and she looked so grown up with the beginnings of a woman's figure forming, but she would have known her anywhere. Her face had not changed; she still wore that excited, wide eyed look.

"Madeleine?" She whispered.

Her hand went to her chest, she took a deep breath and wondered if she were hallucinating.

"Mother!" The child ran to her and she jumped to her feet as her daughter threw herself into her arms and pressed her head as close to her bosom as it could possibly get. She clung to her mother as though afraid she might slip away and as Philippa hugged her back quick tears began to form in her eyes. She moved her a little away and held her face in her hands to kiss her, but her joy was marred by the treacherous thought that if Madeleine was here, something must have happened to her father.

"I don't understand," she said. "Why are you here?"

"Father brought me," she answered in that urgent, breathless voice. "We had to stay at an inn overnight, twice. It was too far to come all in one day and we had to share a chamber, as Father said he would feel I was not safe with just me and Puddle." She stopped talking and looked at the dog, who had lain down on the floor with his chin on his paws. "This is Puddle," she went on rapidly. "I wanted to sleep on the trundle bed that pulled out from under the big one, but Father said it was too close to the floor and there might be rats, so he slept on that with Puddle."

Philippa could only gaze in wonder at her daughter, the idea of Richard sharing a bed with a dog somehow too bizarre to contemplate. But out of all the information Madeleine had poured out for her to sort through, there was one sentence which broke away from the others and raised its solitary voice to be heard: *Father brought me.*

"Your father is here?" She asked in a hoarse whisper, her heart suddenly beating wildly.

"Yes, but he has gone off somewhere. Is that the shawl I embroidered for you?"

Philippa wore the white silk shawl with its tiny embroidered flowers, which Madeleine had sent to her. The shawl was one of the things she wore over her head to cover the ugly scar on her cheekbone. Now she lifted the hem to look at the delicate embroidery, and she nodded.

"It is, thank you. It is beautiful. Everyone admires it."

She hoped the child did not think to ask who everyone was, because in truth her companions were not ones her father would approve of.

"My darling," she murmured and she held Madeleine close once more. "It is so wonderful to see you."

The words seemed a little tame compared to her feelings. She thought her heart might burst with the joy of holding this girl close to her again, of being free to kiss her and hug her and listen to her excited voice, as though she had broken out of her dreams and become real.

"You too." Madeleine lowered her voice but it was clear she was too excited to whisper for long. "I know not why we have come; Father came home from visiting someone and told me we were coming here. I asked no questions in case he changed his mind, but on the way here he told me he had made a terrible mistake. I am not really sure what he meant, but I think that is why we came."

Could it be true, that he realised after all these years that he had made a mistake? And what mistake did he mean, exactly? Was his mistake in not listening, not believing or in accusing her in the first place? She longed to know the answers to these questions, but whatever the answer was, it had caused him to change his mind after all this time and bring her daughter home.

"Do you have all the gifts and things I sent you?" Madeleine was saying in that breathless voice.

"Of course. Do you want to see?"

Madeleine nodded eagerly and took her mother's hand, running her thumb over it affectionately. As Philippa stood, her hair which was carefully arranged in front of her ears fell back a little, pushing the embroidered edge of the shawl with it, and showed the angry scar just in front of her ear, which marred her lovely face. Madeleine put up her hand and stroked the blemish with her fingers.

"What happened?" She asked.

"An accident," Philippa replied. "Just me being clumsy."

She had to lie; she would never want Madeleine to know the truth about the blemish and she had become quite adept at answering that particular question with a lie. They held hands all the way to Philippa's bedchamber where Madeleine looked about in wonder at all the poems, the tapestries, the embroidered scenes she had sent over the years. The wall was almost covered.

"Oh, Mother, you have kept everything." She walked to the far corner and looked up at a picture which she had painted soon after she had arrived in London. It was supposed to be their garden, but she had no talent for art, not like her mother. "You should take this one down. It is not very good."

"No matter. Everything you send me is precious and deserves a place."

She watched fondly as her daughter slowly moved around the chamber, remarking on some of the things she had made over the years. One thing Philippa never expected, not even in her wildest dreams, was that Madeleine would ever see the things she had sent, see them displayed on the walls of her mother's bedchamber.

"I do not remember this one," she said as she stopped before a small picture made of linen and bearing a cross stitched pattern.

"You wrote me you were not well when you sent me that one," Philippa replied. "You had caught a fever from getting wet in the lake. I remember because I was so worried about you and I couldn't…" She was about to remark that she couldn't write to enquire, because she had promised Richard. She caught herself in time. "I am running out of wall space though; I will soon have to move to a bigger chamber."

The voice that came from the open door made Philippa start, made her heart tremor with a mixture of joy and dread upon hearing the familiar but half forgotten deep tones.

"You will not have to," he said. "Madeleine will not need to send you any more things if she is to stay here with you."

They both stared at him for a few moments. Philippa felt a flutter of excitement deep in her stomach, and she could not speak even if she had anything to say, which she did not. Her mind had gone completely blank for a few seconds, before she recalled the fury on his face the last time she had seen him and she closed her eyes against the image.

Finally, it was Madeleine who spoke.

"May I?" She asked, a note of wonder in her voice. "May I really stay here?"

Her brown eyes grew so round and wide they looked like they might pop out of her head and her little mouth formed a round O as she stared at her father as though he had performed some unfathomable magic trick.

"If it is acceptable to your mother," he answered.

He avoided looking at his wife, keeping his attention deliberately on his daughter.

"Of course it is acceptable," Philippa said immediately, her arms going around her daughter's shoulders and drawing her close. "I can think of nothing I would like more except...will you be staying as well, My Lord?"

Even as she asked the question, Philippa was unsure of what answer she wanted to hear. It was still his house and if he wanted to stay in it, that was his decision, but she was not sure she wanted to be here as well, not when he believed her guilty of adultery with his own brother. She could not tolerate that, even though the house was big enough so they need never meet.

"For a few days," he replied, finally letting his eyes meet hers, "then I must return to London. But I will stay in the town if you prefer. I do not wish to impose my presence if it is unwelcome."

He gave Madeleine a quick glance, but she was smiling so much she looked as though she might burst.

"Of course you must stay here," Philippa replied. "It is still your house."

"Can we walk along the beach?" Madeleine asked excitedly.

"Tomorrow," said Philippa. "The tide is coming in now; it would not be safe. Your bedchamber is just as you left it, so you might think it a little childish for such a grown up young lady."

"May I see?"

"Of course. Shall I take you?"

"I think I will find my way." She released her arms from her mother's waist and ran to the door, stopping to hug her father on the way. "Thank you so much," she said to him.

Richard turned and watched her run off toward the stairs which led to the nursery floor, the dog following behind, then called after her.

"If you want any grown up things, you have only to say."

"Thank you," came a voice which faded as it moved further down the gallery to the nursery chamber which Philippa had kept just as she left it. It had become a shrine to her lost child and she had begun to think of it as just that.

She waited until she could hear Madeleine's footsteps reach the top floor, hear the door open and close before she turned to Richard. She half expected a loud and venomous quarrel to ensue once they were alone and she did not want her daughter to hear it.

She was half afraid to be left alone with him, expecting a repeat of their last meeting. But she would be ready this time; she would not be shocked into silence.

"Are you ill?" She asked abruptly.

"No," he replied. "What makes you think so?"

"Either you are ill or you are going to fight some cause for the King. Why else would you entrust Madeleine to my care? I have to be a last resort."

"I am not ill," he answered with a weary sigh, "and I am not going into battle."

He looked nervous, an impression borne out by the trembling in his hands. She wondered why, wondered why she should be so fearsome as to make him nervous. Perhaps he was remembering their last meeting; perhaps he was at last feeling the shame of what he had done to her.

Seeing him again was churning her emotions into a terrifying mix which threatened to tear her apart. Now her memory was showing her his warm smile, his tender kisses, his interest in everything she did. She could not bear it, not when he believed she had betrayed him, not when he refused to listen to the truth. For that she had hated him and still did. She had to drive away the memories before they made her scream.

"Well?" She demanded bitterly. "Why have you come?"

His eyes met hers for a moment, then dropped their gaze to his feet.

"Madeleine is twelve years old," he finally answered. "She needs a mother's guidance."

Instinct told her that was not all, not his only reason for being here.

"She has always needed a mother's guidance," she replied. "What has changed? You are seeking a husband for her?"

"I have made some enquiries, settled some negotiations." He said. "But it is something we have to discuss."

"We?"

"I do believe it to be a decision for us both."

His words pleased her, but she did not trust them. She had always known him so well, always known when he was prevaricating, trying to change the subject for his own ends. She did not believe he had brought Madeleine all this way, after keeping her away since she was little more than a baby, just so her mother could have a say in choosing a marriage partner for her.

The uncomfortable thought flitted across her mind that perhaps talk of the King's divorce had given her husband thoughts of a similar nature. If the King could do it, why not an earl? It would not be an easy thing to achieve, but the King's break with Rome could be to Lord Morton's advantage. He was close to the King, he might well get dispensation from him to divorce his faithless wife and remarry.

Her heart seemed to twist as she thought about it. After their long separation, after the way he had hurt her, she would not have believed she cared, but apparently she was wrong. The thought of him married to someone else made her want to weep.

He would think nothing of putting her through the scandal, would he? He would think nothing of making her name public, but not Madeleine. He would not be talking of finding a husband for Madeleine if his intention was to divorce her mother, surely not. It would be almost impossible to find a good match for her if that happened.

He could find a blood link somewhere if he searched back far enough, he might even invent a previous commitment, although they had been promised to each other since they were children. But he had told Madeleine she was to stay here and he would not lie to her.

Once she was suitably married though, then he would be free to rid himself of his wife by fabricating evidence.

Philippa suddenly thought of her friends and their secret group. They met once a week, usually here, to read and discuss the forbidden texts they kept hidden, the writings of Martin Luther and others like him. Richard would never approve of their meetings. She would have to find some way to deter them whilst he was here, had to stop meeting them for Madeleine's sake. If he found out about her anti catholic studies, she would lose her child again.

Tears had sneaked into her eyes while the thoughts raced through her mind and she turned quickly to the window to wipe them away with her fingers.

"What else?" She asked shakily.

He smiled.

"You know me so well."

She turned back to face him, her anger rising.

"I always did. What a pity you never knew me so well."

She felt her voice begin to tremble as she waited for an answer. Seeing him again after all this time aroused all those feelings she always had for him, despite the beating he had given her before he left, taking her child with him. She would never get over that, never forgive him for that, and she had little hope of forgetting when she was vividly reminded each time she saw her own reflection. He would never have done that had he not been governed by a blind and jealous rage, she knew that, but the knowledge did not make the scar fade, or the hurt, not one bit.

She tried to stop him, tried to keep her distance to give herself time to tell him, but he was as hungry for her as she was for him and he flung his arms around her, much as Madeleine had when she first arrived here just a little while ago. She had so looked forward to seeing him, had missed him so much and needed his comfort as well as his love. He was kissing her, sending those half forgotten chills and tingles through her body, when the illicit foetus chose that moment to move.

He pulled away, gave her a puzzled frown, then placed his hand on her stomach; she flinched at the horror in his eyes when they met hers. She was starting to explain, when he hit her, with the back of his hand so that his heavy ring cut into her face. It was so unexpected she had no time to move out of the way or try to plead with him. He had never been a violent man; he had always treated her with love and respect, he had always had little patience with men who were violent to women. She had no time to recover from the shock before he pulled her roughly to her feet and hit her again, this time with his palm, bruising the other side of her face. He hit her many more times before she fought back in desperation, fearing for her life.

She pleaded with him, called his name, begged him to stop but he seemed not to hear her and she had no alternative but to lash out with her feet, forcing him to release her so she could flee to another part of the house and lock herself in, trembling with fear.

She had lived through that year, worrying about him, knowing he put himself in danger every day fighting for the King, wondering if he would ever return. She had no way of knowing if the war was over, if he was still in France or back in London, on his way home to her.

And during that year, her quiet contentment with her marriage, that special love they had always shared, was destroyed by the horror of his brother coming into her chamber and slipping into the bed beside her.

She woke to feel his fingers on her neck and her dreams followed her for a few seconds; she reached out and caressed his naked chest, thinking it to be her husband about whom she had been dreaming. Then she came fully awake to remember he was miles away in another country. She opened her eyes and gasped, tried to roll over away from him, but he grabbed at her, pulled her back.

"What are you doing?" She demanded. "Let go of me! Get out of here."

"Oh, come on, Philippa. I know you want me; you just showed me that."

"I was asleep. I thought...........I made a mistake. Get out!"

"I saw you two together. You must miss it."

"I miss my husband; that does not mean I want you instead."

She struggled against his grip, but he would not let go. She could scarcely believe this was happening, that Stephen would be doing this. He must have lost his mind. She had never liked him, never trusted him, but seeing how his brother loved him she had kept silent on the subject. She had not been pleased with the arrangements Richard had made for him to look after things during his absence, but there was no one else and she had no valid reason to argue the matter.

"Please, Stephen," she pleaded. "Leave me alone. Richard will never forgive you if you hurt me."

"I have no intention of hurting you," he said. "Just the opposite."

She squirmed, trying to get away from him, but he held on to her, he put both hands on her shoulders and held her firmly to the mattress. She opened her mouth to scream for help and he clamped his hand down on her mouth to silence her. She began to panic then, feeling helpless and weak against his strength. She managed to bite his palm so that he pulled his hand away.

"Stephen! Let go of me."

"I know how you like to be touched," he said, as his mouth came down on her neck. "You must miss it."

"Get off me!"

Then she felt his knee forcing its way between her legs, forcing them apart. She twisted and struggled, but he was too strong for her. She raked her fingernails down his back, digging as hard as she could, but he moved his hands to her wrists and held her arms above her head. She turned her face away and tears sprang to her eyes.

She wanted Richard, not him. Richard would never treat her like this.

Now she dragged her attention back to the present, to gaze at her husband as he stood watching her.

"I came to apologise," he said at last. "And to tell you I know I was wrong. My brother is dead."

"I am very glad to hear it."

"Still as outspoken as ever? That tongue will get you into trouble one day."

"And will you care when it does?"

She could not forget their last meeting. She had suffered a violent attack at the hands of his brother and was longing for his comfort, longing for him to come home and tell her it would all be all right, because that is who he was, a fair, just man who loved her. Instead of his comfort, he blamed her, had beaten her, an act she would never have believed him capable of.

Now she watched him carefully, wondering where this was leading. So he was apologising, because his rapist brother was dead? The two things did not connect in her mind.

"My brother was stabbed by a woman," he went on, "in self defence."

So he had done it again, and now Richard knew the truth, knew that his wife had not been unfaithful, had in fact been the victim of both brothers. She smiled wistfully.

"Ah," she said, "now I see. You believe a total stranger, but not your wife. It is to be expected."

Richard's gaze dropped to look at his feet, ashamed to face her, and he flushed.

"He asked for me when he knew he was dying," he went on. "He told me the truth; he wanted my forgiveness."

She laughed derisively.

"Did he get it?"

"No and he never will. Until he can give us back the years we lost because of him, I will never forgive him, any more than I expect you to forgive me. I was hoping we could put our differences aside for Madeleine's sake."

"What differences, My Lord?" She asked him bitterly. "We had no differences before your lecherous brother attacked me. Did you bother to read any of my letters?"

"All of them. The first one telling me what really happened and I thought you had taken time to invent the tale. I did not believe you." He paused, deep in thought. "The next one which came with the painting of the beach, begging me to allow you to see our daughter. I dismissed the request out of hand. I did not think you were good enough for her."

She caught back a sob that had risen without warning. He thought she was not good enough for her own child. She looked at his expression, wondering if he even considered how his admission made her feel.

"And the last one?"

"The one begging me not to allow our daughter to grow up believing her mother had abandoned her? That was the one that hurt me more than anything, the one that jolted me and made me suggest she send you her gifts."

She had given up sending letters after that. He would allow no letters to Madeleine. Just what he imagined she would say to her child which was unsuitable she could not imagine. She would not lower herself to keep trying to make him understand the truth; she was too hurt that he had thought so badly of her. She did not feel she owed him an explanation, she should not have to explain. He should have known, he should have known her well enough to know the truth, to know she would never be unfaithful to him. She wrote one letter of explanation, she gave him but one chance to believe her. More than that she would not do.

She turned her thoughts back to the gifts her daughter had sent her.

"I thought it was your own idea," she said.

"No," he replied. "It was yours, and she was so pleased when I suggested it, I felt awful for keeping her away from you. But even then I blamed you, told myself that had you been a faithful wife, our daughter would not be without her mother."

She only stared at him, her feelings torn in two. Part of her wanted to throw herself into his arms and love him, feel his flesh against hers once more, while the other part wanted to tear him apart with her bare hands.

"I am deeply sorry," he said. "If I could turn back time and do it all again..."

"You would do no different. You would not believe me, any more than you did then. That is what hurt more than anything else, that you would not believe me. You would not even listen, would not even consider that there had to be another explanation. I thought we were closer than that. I thought you knew how much I loved you, that I could never betray you. If you only knew how horrible that night was, the night he forced himself on me. I was bruised and I felt sick and dirty; I wanted you, not him. Yet you believed I was willing, you even believed I seduced him. How could you?"

"I thought I could trust him," he answered still keeping his distance from her. "I could not believe my brother would force himself on you, I could not believe he was that sort of man. I asked him to look after the estate and to look after you."

She laughed scornfully.

"Well, he certainly got that wrong."

"I was so angry and jealous I could not think straight. And you? I had been gone for a year. You were so passionate, I thought perhaps you needed that passion."

That hurt. That hurt so much, to know that the man she loved thought she could feel that desire for anyone but him. She swallowed the ache.

"Did it never occur to you," she said, "that my passion was only for you? That my desire was only for you? Did you think I was some sort of whore who could give that passion to any man who came along?"

He reached out to her, but she stepped away.

"I did not think that, no," he replied. "I did not think at all. I was just so angry, I lashed out without thinking of anything. I wanted you, I was so looking forward to holding you in my arms, to making love to you, and I came home to find you with child. I was so shocked, I could not think. I just needed to hurt someone, you and him, but he escaped. If only you had written, warned me, given me time to prepare myself."

He looked as though he might burst into tears at any minute and against her will, her heart went out to him. He did not deserve her sympathy, but still she wanted to comfort him.

She laughed derisively as she walked toward the window and looked out at the green and yellow patchwork of the landscape, the little stone cottages scattered about, the familiar sight of the horses moving along the fields. She was rapidly losing the battle to control her emotions; she had believed she would never see Richard again and now this day had come she was in turmoil, not knowing what to do, how to act. She did not know whether to tear off his clothes and make love to him or grab a knife and stab him to death. She wanted to do both.

"Oh, yes," she said, "I was supposed to tell the man I loved, who was risking his life on a battlefield somewhere, that his brother had raped me, his brother who he had trusted to look after me had forced himself on me. Did you think I would risk your life like that? Did you imagine I would want you worrying about me and him and what was happening here, instead of concentrating on keeping yourself alive?"

She turned to find him standing behind her, so close she could smell the masculinity coming from him, could almost hear his heart beating, yet she had not heard his approach. She wore the silk shawl her daughter had made for her and now she held it beneath her chin so it covered the prominent scar on her face. She reached up to pull the two halves closer together, but not before he had seen what was hidden beneath.

He pushed her hair away from her face, keeping his fingers entangled in the soft tresses and he gasped when he saw the angry scar she tried to hide. It was a deep scar, reminding him of a crater in a pool of hard clay, and he remembered that trail of blood which flowed down her cheek, which soaked into the collar of her gown the last time he had seen her.

"Did I do that?" He asked. She made no reply, only stared up at him with resentment in her heart, and she shivered when she remembered that day. "I did," he answered his own question. "How can I ever make it up to you?"

She drew a deep breath to control her rising anger.

"Make it up to me?" She demanded furiously. "Give me back my daughter's childhood; erase seven years of loneliness and misery? Give me back my flawless complexion, my happy life, the man I knew would never hurt me? Make it up to me, just like that?"

She pushed him away, feeling she would hit him if he stayed this close to her.

"You have brought my child home," she went on with difficulty. "Let that be enough."

CHAPTER FOUR

That night they went together to be sure Madeleine was comfortable and happy in her bed, her own little bed which had stood empty since she was five years old. She was really too big to sleep in the nursery suite now, but for tonight keeping her there was a feeble attempt to turn back time.

The child was exhausted, both from the journey and from the excitement of the day and she curled up beneath the covers with a little smile on her pretty face. Puddle lay down beside the bed, ready to guard his young mistress in this strange house.

Philippa stood over her for a few minutes, trying to assure herself that she was really here, that it was no dream. Every day for years she had entered this chamber and looked at that bed, and imagined Madeleine there, beneath the covers, sleeping soundly where she should be. It was hard to believe she really was here at last.

"Goodnight, my love," she said as she leaned over and kissed her. "Tomorrow we will play in the waves and show Puddle how to dig in the sand."

Madeleine laughed then closed her eyes, while her mother watched for a little while longer until Richard put a hand on her waist to guide her away.

"Come now," he said, "let her sleep."

"I will. I just want to be sure she is asleep, that she is content."

What Philippa really wanted was to convince herself that she would not disappear once she left the room. Downstairs in the sitting room, she poured wine for herself and her husband. It seemed so strange to have him here, like a dream which would soon fade and leave her feeling more lonely than before.

"Must you return to London?" She asked. "I mean, so soon?"

He gave her a puzzled frown.

"You speak as though you want me to stay," he remarked.

She made no reply for a few minutes, trying to guess where the conversation might lead.

"Is that so very odd?" She answered at last. "I will not pretend I have not missed you and I would like to hear what you have been doing with yourself."

Her words warmed his heart and he smiled.

"I think it would be best to know what is going on at court. The King has lost his senses over this woman. He is risking war with Spain, he risks putting the whole country under an interdict, excommunicating every living soul and risking his own soul in the process, all because he cannot keep his lust under control."

Philippa handed him the goblet then sat opposite him, just as she used to all those years ago. Sitting like this was like stepping into the past but try as she might she could not recapture those comfortable feelings of closeness that went with it. They had always enjoyed those evenings of discussion, of friendship; they had both looked forward to their time alone in their little room, a roaring fire in the winter. She had not heard talk of this nature for a very long time.

"Is it lust?" She asked him. "Does he not love the Lady Anne?"

"Love? I believe if he ever loved anyone it was Catherine, but the way he is treating her now makes me doubt he is capable of such an emotion. Even if he sincerely believed he was doing his best for the kingdom, as he pretends, he would treat her with more respect if he loved her. He pretends that it is not his choice, that he would keep her as his Queen were it up to him, were God not angry that he had married his brother's widow, but that is not the truth." He sipped his wine and looked at her with familiar animation in his eyes, the sort of excitement he would always have when discussing a subject about which he was passionate. Philippa had not realised how much she missed that.

"He has banished her," he went on. "He has deprived her of her title of Queen, insists everyone refer to her as the Dowager Princess of Wales and he is keeping her away from the Princess Mary, has forbidden her to see her daughter."

She waited for a moment, watching his reaction to his own words, waiting to see if he saw the irony in them.

"Ah, yes," she commented at last, when he said nothing. "I can see where you would disapprove of that."

"I certainly do, I..." He stopped talking and looked at her, his cheeks flushed. "I sound like a hypocrite."

"It did cross my mind."

"I had a good reason," he defended himself. "Or at least I thought I did."

"I imagine the King also believes he has a good reason."

"He is keeping them apart until Catherine admits that their marriage is invalid, that she lied when she swore that her marriage to his brother was never consummated. He is dragging up witnesses to Arthur's boasting the morning after their marriage, when he told everyone he had been deep inside Spain." He laughed scornfully. "The King did not believe it when it suited him, now things have changed and he wants the Queen to admit he spoke the truth. That will be admitting she lied before God and it would be admitting her daughter is a bastard. She will never do it."

Privately, she thought that a very cruel thing to do, just to get his own way, but she said nothing on the subject. She would have agreed to anything to get her daughter back. But she did not want to talk about the King, she wanted to talk about them, about their own situation and what the future held, if indeed it held anything. And she wanted to know about this prospective bridegroom he had found for Madeleine.

She had missed Richard. She would never deny it, despite the injustice with which he had treated her, despite the pain he had inflicted on her, and she still loved him, she always would. She never expected to have him back in her life, thought she would likely go to her grave without ever feasting her eyes upon him again, and now she was unsure whether he wanted to be part of her life again or whether he thought himself better off without her.

And what her own feelings were she could not tell. If he did want to be a part of her life again, she was not sure she would want that. It would be very hard to build a future without the constant reminders of the past.

At last she sighed.

"And you?" She asked him. "What was your reason?"

He flushed again and slowly shook his head, then drained his goblet and stood up, went to the cabinet to pour more wine. At last he replied.

"I believed you to be a whore," he said regretfully, "and I thought you would corrupt our daughter."

She was more surprised than offended. She had not thought that to be his reason.

"If that is true," she said, "then I have been wrong."

He looked surprised, but took his wine back to his seat and sat down, crossing his legs.

"How so?"

"I have always believed you did it to punish me," she answered. "I could never understand why you also wanted to punish Madeleine. I should have known you better than that, but then if anyone had suggested you would ever be violent toward me, I would have laughed in their face."

His eyes met hers for a moment, then moved to look upon her disfigurement. It was not very big, but it was prominent and star shaped, the flesh creased as it folded toward a dip in the centre. It was the inverted shape of the ring he still wore and now she stared at it, at the glittering lights in the ruby as they reflected and bounced off the candles.

He pulled it from his finger and dropped it on the table beside him in disgust.

"Have people asked about it?" He said.

"Some have," she replied. "But you need not concern yourself. I have never told a living soul how I got this scar and I never will."

"Thank you," he answered gratefully.

"I did not keep my secret to protect you," she answered, shaking her head. "I kept it to protect myself, to shelter me from derision and pity. Do you think I want people to know I am still in love with the man who did this to me, who would leave me looking like this?"

He was shocked by her admission, but he said nothing, made no comment on it.

"I will always be ashamed of that," he replied. "Even before my brother told me what he had done, I was ashamed of it. I should have written to beg your forgiveness for that, but I could not bring myself to do it. I would wake from dreams of you, angry enough to kill. I wanted no contact with you at all."

She gave a little smile of satisfaction then felt guilty for it.

"It would seem that these years have given you little peace," she remarked.

But his words did nothing to ease her turmoil. She looked at his handsome face, at his dark hair and fine features, at the strong, firm body she had always loved so much and she longed to hold that body against her own. Her heart had shattered into pieces the day he left, ignoring her pleas, ignoring the blood which poured down her face, and she could do nothing to bring him back, to make him listen. He had not left her enough money to make the journey to London and even if he had, she could not bear to arrive at his London house only to be told she was unwelcome. All she could do was write letters, not knowing if he bothered to read them.

Now she gazed at him and she both loved and hated him, loathed him with a hatred that was strong enough to make her want to kill him, while wanting him as desperately as she ever had, wanting to feel his arms around her, his lips on hers, wanting to feel him inside her. How could she feel this way? It should not be possible to despise this man yet yearn for his touch at the same time. She drew a deep breath to summon the courage to hear the answer to her next question.

"Who is in my place now, My Lord?"

"Sorry?"

"You are not going to tell me you have remained celibate, without the comfort of a woman."

He hesitated for a moment. This was not a subject he had anticipated having to discuss when he came here. If he had expected anything, it had been his words of apology greeted by hers of bitterness. He did not expect to be sitting here opposite her, just as they had in the past, having a perfectly civilised conversation.

"No, I am not," he answered as he swirled his wine about in the goblet, staring at so he would not have to meet her gaze. Now he knew the truth, he felt ashamed of having been unfaithful to her, but it was pointless to deny it; she would know he was lying. She always knew if he was lying. "There have been many women, from all walks of life."

He recalled with no sense of shame how he had dismissed Olivia. He had a reason, an excuse for getting rid of her, but he had dismissed the others just as callously. Whenever they got too close, began to treat him with that familiarity of possession, he would end the affair. He would not risk them coming too close to Madeleine and he would never love any of them; he would not risk his heart again.

All those women had but one purpose and one alone, to drive away the memory of Philippa and what they had shared, to erase the image of her sharing those same things with his brother. But none of them were capable of doing it.

Philippa sat forward to stare at her feet, wishing she had never asked the question. She would not have asked it, had she known the answer would hurt so much.

"Each one occupied your place in bed," he went on, "but not one of them could occupy your place in my heart, in my affections. That place will always be yours."

His words pleased her, eased some of the resentment she was feeling, but she was surprised to hear them just the same. If this conversation followed the path it had begun, someone was going to be seriously hurt and she thought it wise to change the subject.

"Will you support the King in his attempt to become head of the church? It would be dangerous to refuse."

"I have no idea what I will do yet." He sighed heavily. "I only know one thing: I have missed this."

"What?"

"Having someone I can talk openly with without fear of betrayal." He reached across the space between them and took her hand. "We had a good marriage, Philippa. We had the sort of marriage most people only dream about and I allowed Stephen to wreck it. I was fool enough to throw it away."

It seemed she was not to be allowed to change the subject, even though the current one scared her so much she found it difficult to form the words and allow them to escape her thoughts.

"Have you thrown it away?" She asked him.

He made no reply for a few moments, only looked at her intently as though trying to see into her mind.

"You know it is too late for us," he said with regret. "We both know that."

That made her angry again. How dare he come back here after all this time, after keeping her from her child, and decide that he knew her better than she knew herself? She pulled her hand away from his, got to her feet and drained her wine goblet, slammed it down on the mantelpiece, before she replied.

"I have managed a long time without your guidance, Richard," she told him angrily. "Please do me the courtesy of not telling me now what I know."

CHAPTER FIVE

Her words rang in his ears as he watched her run from the room and slam the heavy door. *I am still in love with the man who did this to me.* How could she be still in love with him? Did that mean she could forgive him, that it was not too late for them after all? And even if she could, was it possible he could ever forgive himself? Would his violent outburst and his subsequent actions always hang between them, always be there waiting to step in each time they disagreed? Would she be afraid of him every time he lost his temper, afraid he might strike out at her? He could not live with that, he knew he could not. Could he make love to her again without thinking of Stephen and what he had done, what Richard believed the two had done together? And even if he could, she may not want that; she may see it as a reminder of what his brother had done to her.

He recalled how they used to be together, how they had laughed and loved, walked along the beach holding hands, stopped to kiss and hold each other for no other reason than that they wanted to. He could not believe they could ever have that back; it was gone forever.

And he still had not found the courage to ask her about the child. He could see it was not here, not living in his house, so he could only assume she had fostered it out after all. But he wanted to know her reasons. Was it because she could not bear to raise the child of her rapist? Was it because it was her husband's house but not her husband's child? She might want it back, might want to raise it and if she did, he would support her decision, if only to show her that he still loved her as well.

He caught the thought and held on to it; that was not an admission he was expecting to make, even to himself, but it was true nonetheless. When he arrived that morning and saw her, his heart had skipped. He let Madeleine run off to find her alone, not wanting to spoil their reunion with his presence, which he was sure would be unwelcome, but he had hidden behind a pillar to observe the two of them on the balcony.

How lovely she still was, how serene and gentle and how happy she looked holding her child in her arms. And how ashamed he felt for having kept them apart for so long.

Later when he found them together in Philippa's bedchamber, the chamber he had once shared with her, he had so wanted to fold her up in his arms and hold her close, so wanted to kiss her as he used to, so wanted to lie her down on that bed and love her again.

He caught his breath when she lifted her head and the shawl which covered it fell back, when he saw that scar marring her lovely features for the first time. Even then he failed to associate it with that day, he had not realised that it was he who had caused it. He was even about to ask her what had happened when a memory stopped him, a memory of the last time he saw her, leaning from the open window, clutching a blood soaked cloth to her face and calling out to him, begging him to believe her. The realisation that the scar had been caused by him almost sent him running from the house, never wanting to face her again, so he said nothing about it, pretended he had not noticed it.

But the child? He had to know about the child, yet he could not bring himself to ask her.

There was one other person in this house who would tell him the truth, one he would not hurt with his questions. His nurse, Alice, who had raised him from a baby, had treated him as her own and loved him as her own. He had seen nothing of her all day but then he had not looked. He had not given her a thought and now he wondered if all was well with her. If she was in the house and knew he was home, she surely would have come down to see him, but there had been no sign of her and now he wondered why.

He had been too wrapped up in the wonder of being back here, in the joy of seeing Philippa again, seeing the sheer delight on his little girl's face. He was sure Alice would be about somewhere.

He stopped on his way to the nursery as he recalled that last day and remembered again that Alice had been there, had been in the nursery when he took Madeleine away, when he told the nursery maid to pack up her things ready to leave for good, when he had picked his daughter up and left with her in his arms.

He had forgotten. He had forgotten that she stood in front of him and told him to calm down, to talk to Philippa.

"Richard, you will regret this," she had shouted at him. "Do not do this to your wife and child without all the facts."

He remembered staring at her, uncomprehending, almost as though she spoke a foreign language.

"Facts?" He answered. "I have all the facts I need."

"Richard, listen! You are making a mistake!"

He heard her voice following him as he strode angrily away, but he did not listen. He was too enraged to listen, to consider. There could be no facts but those he already had: his wife was with child by his brother. What else was there to know?

The woman he loved had betrayed him. She had got tired of waiting, needed comfort and had turned to his brother to provide that comfort. He wanted to kill them both.

Now he shook his head to clear his mind and continued on his way to the old nursery where Alice always had her rooms. Even when Richard and Stephen had both grown up and left the nursery, she had kept those rooms.

What the family always referred to as 'the nursery' was in fact the whole top floor of the house, so there were many rooms. Madeleine had her own at the other end of the house, and Alice kept a suite of rooms for herself. He thought she might have moved out, found a more comfortable place on the ground floor to avoid the stairs, but she was still there, still in her familiar surroundings.

Being here again reminded him of his childhood, even made him recapture some of the happy hours he had spent in those rooms, playing with Stephen under the watchful eye of their nurse. He saw little of his parents, but Alice he loved. He had had a happy childhood, had suffered no serious illness, had everything including a good education. There was only one year between him and Stephen and it was only now he paused to wonder why his marriage to Philippa had been arranged so early, but no such thing had been organised for Stephen. It was likely because he was the heir and his parents were anxious to secure a match with a good family.

As he approached the nursery door, he dreaded that he might find signs of Stephen's bastard child in the nursery still, some clothing that he or she had outgrown, something bearing the child's name. He wondered if he had the courage to go and find out. The thought occurred to him that he might even find the child there, that Alice could have hidden it away when she knew he was in the house, which would satisfy his earlier question of why she had failed to come down to see him. The idea disturbed him and he drew a deep breath to give him the courage to face such a child; he could not support his wife in raising her son or daughter if he could not bear to face it.

The elderly nurse still wore the same grey gowns he recalled from his childhood, still wore the same shawls and wore her hair pulled back in a knot at the back of her head, although that hair was almost white where once it had been dark. She seemed to Richard to have shrunk somehow, but that may have been his memory playing tricks on him.

She had been sewing by candlelight and she looked up as he entered, the look in her eyes making him step back as though physically pushed. He could only call it contempt, there was no other word for it.

"My Lord," she said in greeting, making no attempt to get to her feet.

Hearing his title from this woman's lips stopped him coming any closer. She always called him by his given name, always, never 'My Lord'. She was like a mother to him, more of a mother than his own had ever been with her busy schedule and her balls and visits at court.

Alice was getting old and frail, but he thought it more likely to be lack of respect rather than lack of mobility which kept her seated.

"Alice," he said. She did not smile, only stared contemptuously at him, her glance sweeping him. He took a deep breath, cringing inwardly before her disapproval. "It seems I am not welcome in your nursery," he commented, keeping his distance.

He glanced quickly about and was relieved to see no child, nor any sign of one.

"No," she replied insolently, "you are not. But it is your house so I must accept your presence or who knows but you might turn me out into the street."

Her words jolted him. He had come here expecting to grovel to Philippa, but he never expected such harsh words from this woman. He had in fact not thought about her at all, but if he had he would have expected her usual fondness.

"Alice," he protested. "You know I would never do that."

"Do I? I knew you would never hit a woman. I knew you would never keep your child away from her mother. I knew you would never break Lady Philippa's heart." She paused and glared at him. "It would seem I did not know as much as I thought. I knew your brother as well, knew he was a decent man; seems I was wrong about him too. What did I do to the pair of you?"

"Please, Alice," he said, pulling up a chair beside her. "I made terrible mistakes, I know that, but I cannot do anything to change them now. I have to know what happened to the baby."

She looked at him with that same contempt in her eyes, a look that made him shudder, but still he had to know.

"Tell me, please. What happened to the baby?" He persisted.

"What baby, My Lord?"

He sighed impatiently and bit his lip in an attempt to control his mounting temper.

"Just because you raised me does not give you leave to challenge me. When I left here my wife was with child. What happened to it?"

Her eyes met his defiantly and for just a moment he thought she might refuse to answer him.

"Why do you not ask her?" She finally replied.

"I cannot. I cannot bear to hear about it from her own lips. Besides, I have hurt her enough; I fear that talking about it might hurt her more and I do not want that."

"That is something to your credit I suppose."

He drew a deep breath to control his frustration. Why could the woman not simply answer his question?

"When I came here," he said, "I expected my wife to refuse me her forgiveness. I never expected to have to beg for yours."

"I am ashamed of you, Richard," Alice said, her voice rising in anger. "I heard you that day, I heard her screams, I heard you shouting and I heard her fall to the floor where you sent her. I can never describe how shocked I was; I thought someone had broken in and attacked Her Ladyship. When I realised it was you I could not believe it. I thought I had raised a decent man, a man who knew how to respect a woman."

"You did," he told her. "But I was so angry. I came home after a whole year away to find her with child! How do you think I felt?"

"Very bad I imagine," she said, "but not as bad as her, not as bad as learning that the man she loved was not only violent, would actually attack her, but was not even prepared to listen, to give her time to explain. That you thought she would ever be unfaithful to you, that hurt her more than the beating, more than anything except you stealing her child away." She paused and stared at him, but her expression was no softer. "After being violated by a man she did not want, needing the comfort of the one man she loved, what did she get? Abuse and violence and blame. I wanted to go to London myself, but she would not allow it. She said if you could not realise for yourself what you had done, she did not want you back."

He felt her words stabbing into his heart like a knife. Philippa had been right as well; he was not worthy her forgiveness, not worthy of her love. But still he had to know.

"She never liked Stephen," Alice went on. "Did you know that?"

He shook his head.

"She never said anything against him."

"Not to you, no, because she knew you loved him. But she never liked him; she told me he made her feel uncomfortable, he was always leering at her and at the serving girls. She was not happy when you went off and left him in charge."

"I asked him to look after her," he murmured.

"She told me," Alice replied. "She said you may as well have left her in the care of a pack of wolves."

He closed his eyes and shuddered, wishing for the second time that day that he could turn back time.

"Please, Alice, tell me," he asked her again. "What happened to the baby?"

"Why does it matter so much?" She demanded. "He was not your son."

Now he could feel himself losing control of his temper, although he would never lose it completely, not like the last time he was here.

"It matters to me, because it matters to her," he told her. "At least I suppose it must matter to her. She is not a woman who can simply abandon a baby, no matter the circumstances, and if she should want to be a mother to him, I want her to know I will support her."

Alice's expression softened at last, and her mouth creased a little in sorrow.

"I saw no baby, My Lord," she told him. "I saw a bloody, mangled lump of flesh, but I saw no baby."

Her words left him speechless. In all his speculating about whether she had kept the child or fostered it out, it had never once occurred to him that she might have miscarried. Now as he remembered his rage, how he had hurt her, he knew who was to blame.

"She lost it?" He whispered. Alice nodded and he gradually began to see what he should have seen before. "Because of me?"

"I am no midwife or physician, but I would say that is a fair wager."

"God!" He buried his face in his hands, just long enough to let the information penetrate his thoughts.

He had no idea when the child was due to be born, but as the months went by and he sequestered himself in London, he had thought of her giving birth. He had imagined it to be like Madeleine's birth, that she would be cared for by midwives and she would be happy to be having Stephen's child. It never occurred to him that it would be torture for her, that she was having the child of rape. All he had felt was jealousy that it was not his child; it never entered his head that the violence with which he had treated her would have caused a miscarriage. He had been unbelievably selfish to not even consider the possibility. He had not only attacked a woman, he had attacked a pregnant woman. What sort of monster did that make him?

"It was likely for the best," Alice was saying. "I cannot think what would have become of the little mite, his father run off like the depraved coward he was, his mother branded a scarlet woman, living under sufferance in the house of a man who despised him. Yes, it was likely for the best."

He hardly knew how to ask his next question. He was sure Alice would treat it with more contempt, more scorn, and she was likely right.

"Did she ask for me?" He said at last. "When she was..............when she lost the baby, when she went through that alone; did she ask for me?"

Alice's eyes met his and that contempt returned.

"What do you think?" She asked him in an icy voice. "Who else would she have wanted when she was in pain, when she thought she might die? She asked for you, yes, she cried out for your comfort, for your love, but she would not let me send for you despite that. She wanted you to come back on your own, she wanted you to realise she needed you; she wanted you to realise what you should have known all along - that she would never have wanted another man. That was never going to happen though, was it? Why are you here now? Because Madeleine is almost a woman and you have no idea what to do with her?"

"I came because Stephen is dead and he told me the truth before he died," Richard answered. "So it seems Philippa will never have her wish. I can never give her the one thing she wants now, for me to realise for myself what a bloody fool I was."

Alice said nothing for a few minutes but Richard felt her eyes on him. He knew she was trying to decide on her next words, he knew her well enough to know the signs. There was more to tell and she was not sure if it was her place to tell it.

At last she took a deep breath.

"You cannot even give her the other thing she wants," she remarked bitterly.

"What?"

"Another child."

He stood up and went to stare out of the window, although there was nothing to see. It was dark and there was not even an occasional light from the workers' cottages.

Would she want another child with him? After Madeleine there had been two miscarriages and both times she had been heartbroken. He had been there for her then, but would she want to risk it again? He thought it unlikely she would even want him again.

"I would if she would give me another chance," he said. "But I can never ask that of her."

"That is not what I meant," Alice told him. "You cannot give her another child because your brother's bastard tore her apart, ruined her."

He turned back to stare at her in stunned silence.

"She can have no more babies, Richard, because of the brutality you inflicted on her. You left her with a bloody face and a bloody womb, as well as a heart shattered to pieces. I thought we would lose her for a while; she was so very ill and she had lost the will to live. She had lost you and she had lost her child, the only child she could ever have. But still she insisted I was not to send for you. Between you two fine gentlemen I was so proud of, you managed to crush a good woman and tear her life apart. Congratulations."

CHAPTER SIX

Philippa sat at the table, waiting impatiently for her daughter to join her, hoping her husband had not reconsidered his decision to come here. This morning when she awoke she remembered to send an urgent message to her friends, telling them to stay away until they heard from her. They would wonder, they might even send someone to be sure of her safety, but they knew the danger of ignoring such a warning. She felt better now that was done and she waited to hear those urgent footsteps, and the distinctive padding and panting of the dog following them.

In truth she had no idea how Richard would react if he learned of the group to which she belonged. There were only six of them, ordinary people who had noticed each other and come together because of the pamphlets a preacher was giving out in the market square before he was arrested and taken roughly away.

They each noticed how others reacted to the literature, if they stood and read them or threw them away in disgust, or as in the case of Philippa and the others, they folded them up and hid them away to study in private.

They managed to get hold of some books and papers and they gathered to study and discuss them in secret.

Often they would meet in the ancient hall beside the house, a building that had stood for centuries but was no longer in use. None of them knew that Philippa was Lady Morton. They knew only her first name, her given name and that is how she wanted it. They assumed she was a servant in the house and she never wanted to disabuse them of that assumption. It was far safer for all of them if they knew nothing of her real identity or of the life she once had.

While she enjoyed their studies and believed them to be important, she knew they were dangerous and accepted she would have to give them up now her daughter was home. What they were doing was heresy, the penalties for which were harsh and she would never put Madeleine's safety at risk for any reason. Nothing was as important as her daughter.

She was jolted out of her contemplation by the happy, breathless voice calling a name she had not heard in years before yesterday.

"Mother!" Madeleine ran into the dining hall and flung her arms around her mother's neck, then sat down beside her. Philippa felt those choking tears again, tears of joy and incredulity that this girl was actually here under her roof, sitting beside her, hugging her.

She piled a platter high with bread and cheese and put it on the floor for the dog. "Is it all right for Puddle to eat here with me? He will be happier if he can see me."

"Of course it is all right," Philippa replied with a smile, "as long as he has been outside this morning."

Madeleine nodded, then filled another platter for herself.

"Can we walk along the beach this morning?" She asked excitedly. "The tide is not coming in now."

"Of course we can, darling. I promised, did I not?"

"Can Father come?"

What a strange question to be hearing in this house after all this time.

"Of course he can, if he wants to. It is his house, his beach."

"He does want to; I already asked him."

"Then why are you also asking me?"

"He said I had to be sure it was acceptable to you. Puddle will love the waves."

"He will," her mother replied. "He is going to get very, very wet."

Madeleine was thoughtful for a little while as she ate then she looked up at her mother with a flushed face.

"Why do you and my Father live all those miles apart?" She asked. "Why have I not seen you for such a long time?"

Philippa had no answer. She searched her mind for a suitable response, one which would satisfy the child's curiosity without revealing the truth. She must never know the truth.

"We quarrelled," she said at last. "It was not meant to last this long."

"I know you quarrelled," she said. "I heard you. I remember that day, I remember it very well. I remember how scared I was; there was a lot of screaming and even Alice shouted at Father. I heard you crying."

It had never occurred to Philippa that Madeleine had heard, might still remember. She must have been so frightened. She wondered if Richard knew she remembered, she wondered what he had told her. Philippa reached out a hand and clasped her daughter's.

"Oh, darling, I am sorry. We never wanted you to be frightened."

"I thought it was my fault," she said. "I asked him if I had done something terrible and that was why I was not allowed to see my mother again. I thought I had made you cry."

Philippa got to her feet and went to kneel beside her daughter's chair.

"No, darling, do not ever think that."

"I know that now. He told me it was nobody's fault, that you just did not love each other any more. He would tell me nothing else."

"He said that?"

Madeleine nodded as she chewed her bread.

Philippa got to her feet, not wanting Madeleine to see the tears those words had brought with them.

"I might tell you about it when you are grown up," Philippa said.

"How grown up is grown up? Two of the girls at my school are already betrothed."

"Your school?"

"Yes. I wrote you about it. I go to a school for young ladies of the nobility and we learn all sorts of things. There are only five of us and we meet in each other's houses. We learn all about where different countries are and history. We learnt how the King's father came to the throne, and we learn embroidery and sewing - I am the best of all at sewing."

"I imagine you are," Philippa replied as she lifted the edge of her shawl and studied the delicate embroidery. "What else do you learn?"

"We do painting as well. I showed them my painting of the beach here which you made for me. I told them my mother painted it but then they wanted to know why you did not live with me and I wished I had not shown them."

"It must have been hard for you. Did you tell your father?"

She shook her head.

"He would only be upset," she answered. "We learn lots of things. We learn all about God and the saints."

Philippa's heart sank. Of course it would be a catholic teacher and her child would be learning all about the idols and the relics, the transubstantiation of the Holy Eucharist, about purgatory. All the things she and her friends had rejected as nonsense. She realised she would have to tread very carefully lest Madeleine should learn of her beliefs; if Richard ever found out, he would take her back to London and away from her mother again.

"Anyway," Madeleine went on, "two of my friends are already betrothed, already have marriages arranged. Is that why Father brought me here? Has it something to do with finding me a husband."

"No, darling. He brought you here because he decided we had best put our differences aside for your sake. We will discuss a marriage, but we have a lot of things to talk about concerning our own situation for now."

"How did you meet my father?"

Philippa smiled reminiscently as she tried to recapture the events of her youth, of her wedding. This was just the sort of conversation she should have been having with her daughter, just the sort of thing she needed to know about and she felt suddenly grateful to her husband for bringing her back to her, so she could teach her all these things. That feeling brought anger with it, though. She was angry that she should feel grateful for the privilege of having her child back, when he was the one who stole her away and she should never have lost her in the first place.

"It was arranged for us by our parents," she answered.

"You had never met?"

"No. I had a miniature of him and he had one of me. We wrote letters to each other, which I kept. He kept his too so I have them all together. Would you like to read them?"

Madeleine's eyes grew round with excitement.

"Oh, yes please! May I?"

"If your father agrees, I see no reason why not. We will ask him later, when we have had our walk on the beach."

The dog lifted his head at mention of the word 'walk' and they both laughed. Philippa felt that this was the happiest day of her life, to sit here with her child, tell her all about herself and her father, laugh together.

"In a minute, Puddle," Madeleine assured him, then turned back to her mother. "You did not meet until the marriage itself?"

"We did not."

"Then what happened?"

Madeleine had finished her breakfast and now she half turned in her seat and looked at her mother expectantly, eager to hear the answer to her question.

"Well, I was just fourteen years old, he was two years older. We were very innocent, very naive. We had a sumptuous feast, and dancing, then we were put to bed by drunken guests, flowers were strewn all over the covers, and the priest came to bless the marriage bed. That part was very embarrassing, all those people making suggestive remarks. I was so relieved when they had gone."

"Were you afraid?"

"Yes," her mother replied indulgently. "So was he."

"What happened then?"

Philippa vividly recalled that first time, the first time for both of them. She wore her silk, embroidered shift which she had worn beneath her wedding gown, pale blue for purity. He wore his silk shirt. They had lain together, just staring up at the ceiling except for the surreptitious glances she cast his way. His hand found hers and held it tightly and she could feel the warmth emanating from his body, making her more nervous, then at last he shyly leaned across and kissed her hesitantly, as though afraid she might break. She enjoyed that kiss, so much so that she leaned forward for another one, this one longer and deeper as though he was trying to drink her in. Although it was his first time, he knew how to kiss, knew how to make her melt into his arms as though their bodies were fused together. She knew nothing, and she never asked him if he had known before or if it came naturally. It certainly seemed to.

For the few days that the feasting lasted they talked formally before the guests, while in private they could not wait to repeat that first time, but on the second night they were not accompanied by guests or the priest, they were alone and once inside the bedchamber, he turned and locked the door.

He stood in front of her and untied the ribbons of her shift, slipped it away from her shoulders and let it drop to the floor. She unfastened his shirt and slipped it off and they both swept their eyes over each other, he studying a female form for the first time in his life, she doing the same to him. Being naked together was frowned on by the church, which is why he had locked the door, but it felt right somehow. It was as though they were made for each other, bound together by far more than the words of the priest, but by some ethereal ribbon that would never let them part.

There had never been anyone else for either of them, not until the awful night when Stephen had come into her bedchamber while she slept and raped her. Then the dreadful day Richard had come home from a war to find his wife with child by his brother. Stephen ruined everything, destroyed that special exclusiveness for both of them.

She realised that her daughter was still eagerly awaiting an answer.

"Then we became one with each other, we loved each other," she answered at last. "And the more we knew of each other, the more we loved each other."

"Then something went wrong," Madeleine remarked in a surprisingly adult voice. "Did you try to make things better? Did you write to try to make things better?"

"Yes, I did," she answered then wished she had not. Now Madeleine might blame her father for the wasted years and she did not want that. Although she blamed him and was still angry with him, she never wanted anything to spoil that special bond Madeleine had with her father.

It was unusual for a father and daughter to be so close, especially a father and daughter of the nobility. Very often daughters were merely pawns in a game which was all about property and money. Although Philippa knew her husband would never think of his daughter in that way, she believed their closeness had a lot to do with his sole guardianship of their child and that filled her with resentment.

His voice from the doorway brought relief. At least she would be spared more awkward questions.

"Father," Madeleine jumped to her feet and ran to him. "Mother says she would love you to come with us."

Those had not been Philippa's precise words and she wondered if she had a little matchmaker in the house.

"Then what are we waiting for?" He answered her. "It is a lovely day and Puddle is longing to try out the waves."

Madeleine ran through the door and the dog followed her, while Richard held out his hand to his wife, but she took it reluctantly. She wanted no physical contact with him until she knew if anything could come of this visit, or if he would return to London and think no more about her. The warmth of his grip made her breasts tingle. It had been so long since she felt her flesh against his in any way, she thought she might break down and she knew that if he stayed here for much longer, she would find it difficult to resist him. The anger was still there, hovering beneath the surface of that yearning, wanting to hurt him as he had hurt her. She was torn in two and she had no way of knowing which way to turn.

While Madeleine and Puddle raced toward the waves they began to walk slowly along the beach, keeping a close eye on the sea to be sure their daughter was safe. Philippa wanted desperately to find something to talk about, but every subject filled her with trepidation. She had never felt awkward with him before, but now it seemed that everything she said would lead to resentment she could not conceal.

The sun shone down on her back and the breeze coming from the ocean tossed her skirts about and sent her hair blowing around her face, exposing the scar she had carefully covered up. It did not matter; he knew what he had done. Let him see, let it be a reminder to him each time his eyes fell on her face. It was what he deserved.

"Alice told me about the baby," he said at last, making her heart sink. She wanted to talk, but not about this; this could only lead to more heartache.

"I would rather not talk about it, Richard," she said. "It was the most painful time of my life, in more ways than one." She paused and looked at him with derision in her eyes. "And where were you?" She added angrily. "Sulking in London, feeling sorry for yourself."

The anger had won the battle.

"I am so sorry," he said. "I will not ask you to forgive me, because I shall never forgive myself, but I am sorry and I want you to know that."

She said nothing, but allowed her hand to slip away from his. A seagull flew too close and she ducked out of the way, tumbling into him as she did so and as he caught her to keep her from falling her heart leapt. The unaccustomed warmth of his body was so welcome, she wanted to hold him against her, wanted to feel his heart beating against hers, but she pulled away from him, resisting that closeness, afraid to risk it.

"Alice said you would not let her send for me," he said. She made no reply. "Why?" He asked at last.

"I did not want your pity," she answered bitterly. "I did not want you coming all this way because you felt sorry for me." She paused thoughtfully, then went on. "And I was too afraid you would not come. If Alice had written, told you she feared for my life, and you refused to come, you did not care enough to come, I think I would have died there and then."

They heard a scream and both turned toward Madeleine whose scream was one of delight as she jumped over the waves with her dog, soaking her clothes.

"Why did I not do this years ago?" Richard said regretfully. "Look how happy she is."

"If you had never heard Stephen's confession before he went to Hell where he belongs, you would not be here now," she answered bitterly.

He carried on walking, knowing she was right, knowing how close he had come to missing that confession. Had he not been told it was a woman who stabbed him, he likely would have refused to go and see him on his death bed, would never have known the truth. He could not feel worse than he did right now, watching his daughter so happy, his wife so sad, so lost.

"What else did Alice tell you?" She asked him abruptly.

She wondered if the elderly nurse had told him about her inability to conceive. She had decided to keep it to herself unless the subject came up, but she was suddenly afraid of how he would react to her barren condition and she wondered where that fear had come from. After all, they were no longer man and wife in the true sense, so what difference did it make?

"She told me you could have no more children," he answered quietly.

He stopped walking and turned to look down at her compassionately and she felt bitter again. He was pitying her barren state, he who had been the cause of it.

"If you want to be rid of me, free yourself to take another wife," she said angrily, "I will not quietly retire into oblivion, even if you can find evidence, even if you do have the support of the King. I just want you to know that before you start making plans."

He looked stricken for a moment before he replied.

"Why on earth would you think that?" He said.

"We have no marriage, we are no longer of one flesh and even if we were, I cannot give you a son."

She had not noticed the tears in her eyes but he had. His put his hand on her cheek and gently brushed them away with his thumbs, while his fingers touched the scar which marred her lovely features. He tried not to react, but the feel of that scar sent a shiver down his spine.

She made no move to remove herself from his touch. Although the feel of his fingers exploring the scar made her anger seethe, feeling his warm hand on her face was welcome, caused that gentle throbbing deep inside, from wanting him. She wished she could be one thing or the other, not torn in two directions like this. She could not cope with not knowing whether she loved him or hated him.

Loud and excited barking drew their attention and they looked across to see their daughter disappear beneath the waves. They ran, but stopped and watched as she climbed to her feet, laughing so much she could not stand up straight.

"Time to go inside, I think," he said, then went to the shore to tell Madeleine.

She came running up the beach to Philippa, her father close behind her, holding her skirts in her hands and wringing water from the fabric.

"Can I see those letters when I am dry, Mother?"

"Letters?" Richard asked with a frown.

"I forgot to ask you," Philippa said as they made their way back toward the house. "You remember the letters we wrote to each other before we were wed?" He nodded. "I told Madeleine she could read them, if that meets with your approval."

"Really?"

Philippa could see he was reluctant and she turned to her daughter.

"Madeleine, hurry inside and get yourself and Puddle dry. We will be along in a moment."

They watched her go then she turned to him.

"If you do not want her to see them," she said, "I am sure she will understand."

He made no reply for a moment, as though trying to recall what secrets he might have given away all those years ago.

"No, it is all right," he answered with a frown. "I am surprised that is all."

"There is nothing untoward in them, nothing intimate. They were written before we ever met." She stood and studied his reaction. "I thought with talk of her own marriage, she might gain some knowledge from them, that they might help her to understand how two people who had never met could be happy together."

Once more her own words had caught at her heart, taken her by surprise. They were happy together once, before Stephen had violated his brother's trust and ruined everything. She had not been happy since, but she never wanted Madeleine to know that.

He smiled at last.

"Of course. I am being foolish."

"Why, Richard? Why do you not want Madeleine to read them?"

He drew a deep breath and turned to watch his daughter disappear into the house with her dog.

"I suppose I clung to the hope that they were private, special to us, not for the eyes of others."

She did not expect that. After everything that had happened between them, who would have imagined he still thought those letters to be special?

"Forgive me," she said. "I will tell her."

"No," he argued. "Let her read them. She is part of us."

Madeleine was so exhausted at supper she very nearly fell asleep eating it. Alice came and helped her to bed and she smiled and curtsied to Philippa, but still had no good word or sign of respect for Richard. All he got from her was a scowl.

"It seems I will never have her forgiveness either," he remarked.

"Either?" Philippa asked.

"I mean I will never have the forgiveness of either of you."

She stared at him in silence for a few moments, his words having irked her again.

"Did I miss the part where you asked for forgiveness, Richard?" She said, that anger brimming to the surface again. "In the years since you left here, did you never once think you might have made a mistake? Did you never once think you might be wrong?" He shook his head. "I can almost understand how the shock and anger could make you behave as you did, but you had seven years to think about it, to realise there had to be another explanation."

"I did not want to think about it," he answered. "I shut it out of my mind. It was the only way I could function."

"Did you read the letter I wrote you, telling you what happened? Did my words mean nothing?"

"Philippa, what can I say?" He reached across the table and held her hand. "By the time that letter arrived I was thinking you would have written straight away had you been innocent. I had no way of knowing you were so ill, that you could not write." He paused for a moment, then shook his head before he went on. "That letter made me even angrier if you really want the truth. I thought you were besmirching Stephen's name for your own ends; I could not believe my brother could be a rapist."

Snatching her hand away she leapt to her feet. She glared at him, as though wanting her eyes to stab knives into him, and struggled to get the words out through a massive ache in her throat, through unshed tears which brimmed and threatened to crease her lips and halt her tongue.

"But you had no problem believing your wife, who adored the very dirt beneath your feet, could be unfaithful to you!" She shouted. "You had no problem believing that bedding another man was easy, because I was so passionate?" Her voice rose almost to a shriek and she struggled to control it, afraid that Madeleine would hear. "You had no problem believing me to be a whore who would give herself to the first man who would have her!"

"Philippa, please..."

He still sat, looking up at her, desperately wanting to go to her, to hold her in his arms, to comfort her, but afraid of making things worse.

"When I was waiting for your return," she interrupted him, "I thought about how I would tell you, and one of the worst things for me was that I knew you would be hurt. I would have done almost anything to avert that; I even hoped you might not come home until after the birth, so that you would never have to know, never be hurt. And yes, I hoped to lose the baby, but only so you would never have to know what a depraved deviant your own brother was. My mistake was in expecting you to sympathise, expecting you would show compassion for what I suffered. I never thought I had to hide myself from you, not ever, because it never once crossed my mind that you might think I had willingly bedded another man, any other man."

He opened his mouth to speak, but she put up a hand to stop him.

"When I saw you had felt the child move, I was relieved. I was actually relieved and I expected your first question would be to ask who had done that to me." She paused to gather her emotions under control. "I thought about how it would be," she went on, "how you would turn your brother out, how you would comfort me and assure me things would work out, like you always did about everything. I imagined we would talk about it, decide together what was the best thing to do. That is what we had, do you remember? That is what we always had, that openness, that special bond, but instead you blamed me. You lashed out at me and I was so shocked I thought at first I must have imagined it, until I felt the blood seeping into my collar, until you pulled me up and hit me again."

He got to his feet and strode quickly toward her, reaching out to touch her, but she brushed him away.

"Sweetheart, I..."

"When you felt that movement, your first thought should have been 'my wife is with child; she must have been raped', but instead your first thought was 'my wife is with child, she must be a whore'."

He flinched, genuinely hurt by the venom in her words and the realisation that she was right.

"You gave me no chance to explain," she went on, her voice rising. "You assumed I had been unfaithful to you, when you should have known that could never happen. That is what hurt so much."

She did not want to shed tears before him, did not want him to know how much he had hurt her. She turned and ran from the dining hall and to her bedchamber where she undressed and climbed into the massive bed.

She always made a point of wearing clothes she could get in and out of herself and she was never more glad about that than she was that night. She did not want anyone to see the state to which he had reduced her, just by being here. She wanted time to think, think about how his presence in the house had reduced her to a confused wreck who had no idea what she wanted or how she felt.

Later, when she lay beneath the covers, trying to sleep, trying to banish the memories, the good ones along with the bad, the door opened slowly.

"May I come in?" He asked.

No! She wanted to scream. *Go away!*

"It is your house," she answered.

He approached the bed and sat, looking down at her. He took her hand and kissed her fingers, bringing a memory of the first time he had ever done that, on their wedding day, as they stood before the priest and said their vows. She swallowed a sob.

"I will begin the journey back to London tomorrow," he told her.

Despite her bitterness, her heart sank.

"So soon? You said you would stay until the end of the week."

He sighed heavily.

"I did, but now I realise it will be too hard for both of us. You are not happy with me here; I am just a reminder of what I did to you, and I am finding it intolerable, seeing the hatred in your eyes. I deserve it, too, and that only makes it harder. I cannot live under the same roof with you and not be with you, not be a part of you. I thought I could, but it is too hard."

She fought to suppress the ill feeling, the resentment, but it was almost impossible.

"There is no hatred in my heart for you, Richard," she replied. "Resentment yes, a need for revenge even, but no hatred. I have loved you since the day we met and that has never changed."

He squeezed the hand that he held, brought it to his lips and kissed it once more.

"Thank you for that," he said. "I do not deserve it. Seeing you again is hurting me far more than I expected. It is so hard for me to see you, to touch you, but not have you in my arms."

His words produced that little tingle of passion deep inside that she had not responded to since he went away to fight King Henry's war. She had been feeling that pulsing all day, each time she saw him, each time he held her hand or spoke to her. And he was finding it difficult to resist her? She was not sure if she wanted him to know she felt exactly the same. She wanted him, wanted him desperately, wanted to feel his bare chest pressing against her breasts, wanted to feel his lips on her body, his hips on hers.

Yet her anger refused to release her, would not simply step aside and allow her desire to the surface, leave her free to respond to that pulse of passion.

"Well," she said, "what is stopping you? I still belong to you; you still have the right. Take me, why not? Ease your frustration."

"If that were all it was I could go and hire some whore for the night," he said bitterly.

"What then?"

"You. It is a need for you, no one else. I have put myself through hell; in every woman I took to bed I searched for you, I wanted you. No one else would do or ever will."

He pushed himself up, about to stand and leave her, but she gripped his hand to stop him.

"You want me?" She asked. "You really want me, only me, no one else will do?"

"More than anything."

"Why did you not know that is how I felt, that only you would do? Why did you think I could feel that ardour for anyone else? How could you doubt how much I loved you? That is what I could never understand, that is what hurt so much. I worshipped you. Why did you not know that?"

"I have no excuse, Philippa," he answered. "I was too shocked and angry to think of anything; all I knew was you were having a child and it could not be mine, you had bedded my brother whilst I was away. I never stopped to think, to tell myself that you would never do that. My world was collapsing and I thought I could do nothing to salvage it. Now it is too late."

"So that decision is to be yours alone, is it?" She demanded.

"What do you mean?"

"That is the second time you have told me it is too late. You are so sure of that I can only imagine you want it to be true."

"Of course not!" He argued. "But I have no right to want anything where you are concerned. Tell me to leave and I will go. This will never be my home as long as you do not want me here. I have stolen everything else from you, allow me to let you keep your home as sanctuary from me."

She lay looking up at him, still feeling torn between two passions, love and hatred. It made no sense to her that she had been sick with misery for seven years, misery that he had caused, yet she still wanted him.

"I need no sanctuary from you, Richard," she said, "unless you plan to hit me again."

He gave a shuddering sigh and glanced at his fingers where they intertwined with hers.

"I cannot give you back what I have stolen," he said. "It seems there is nothing I can give you that you might want."

Her eyes met his and she studied his face for a moment. She knew she needed him, wanted him as she had in the past, but she was afraid she would still hate him afterwards.

"There is one thing I want," she finally said.

"Anything," he answered. "If there is anything in the world I am able to give you, it is yours. You have but to name it."

"When I wake in the night, I want to reach out and not feel that empty place where you should be."

He frowned, unsure of what she was saying, knowing what she was saying but knowing he must be wrong.

"What are you telling me, Philippa?" He asked.

"Stay with me tonight," she said softly. She reached up to touch his cheek. "Share my bed, let me feel your arms around me, let me feel your comfort in the night when I awake from bad dreams."

She was very scared of those dreams, those dreams of that day when he had left with her daughter and never returned. She would wake in the dark, reach out a hand to find that empty place and realise those dreams were not dreams at all, but memories. Then she would sob until she cried herself back to sleep, exhausted and desolate.

"You have bad dreams?" He asked her now, "what about?"

She made no reply.

"I too have bad dreams," he said. "I would enjoy your comfort when they wake me."

He laid down on the bed beside her and took her into his arms, her head against his chest. They laid together for a few moments, her arms wrapping themselves around him and holding that strong body close, then she unfastened his shirt and parted it, revealing his bare chest. She slipped her hand inside and ran her fingers over that chest, as she had been longing to do all day, then she turned her head and kissed it, feeling that passion deep inside her again as she intertwined her fingers in his.

He gazed down at her, afraid to believe what his senses were telling him. Did she really think they could have a future together or was this some sort of vengeance? And he realised with a jolt that he was doing her yet another disservice, that she was not given to vengeance and even if she were, she would not use him to attain it.

"I would give anything in the world if we could be together again, anything."

She pulled the hand she still held towards herself and held it at her breast until he began to caress that breast, then he leaned forward and kissed her with all the pent up passion he had suppressed for so long. That passion was hers alone, never for those other women, only hers.

She pulled his shirt out of his waistband.

"Take off your clothes and come and join me," she whispered. "I need you. I have needed you since our very first time together, when neither of us even knew what that meant, and nothing that happened has dampened that."

He was silent for a few moments, while his mind tried to process her words. She was telling him she wanted him, she really wanted to share her body with him, to share his. It was the last thing he expected when he came to say goodnight.

"Really?" He murmured. "You really want me?"

"I want you," she said. "I want you so much I will burst from it."

He took off his clothes and climbed into the bed beside her. His hand slipped inside her shift and caressed her breast, making her gasp, and she recalled vividly how they always slept naked in the past, always enjoyed each other with nothing between them.

"Take it off," she said. "We never needed cloth between us."

He unfastened her shift and slipped it off her shoulders and down, leaving her naked, and pulled her towards him. He took her breast into his mouth, making her pant with desire and move seductively, then his mouth moved up to her neck while she ran her fingers over his nipples, moved down and kissed his chest. Her rapid and heavy breathing was causing him to stir in a way he had never done with all those other women and he remembered that she was the only one who could do this, who could make him feel like this.

He moved down the bed to kiss the inside of her thigh, to breathe into that secret place and make her shiver till she thought she would explode. She clutched frantically at his shoulders, drawing him towards her so she could whisper in his ear.

"Take me!" She said in a husky voice. "Take me now, Richard, please! I can wait no longer!"

The strength of him inside her was something she had dreamed about for years, something she thought she would never have again, and now he moved inside her until she cried out.

Once spent, he kissed her deeply and rested on his elbows to look down at her lovely face with a contented smile before he rolled away and gathered her into his arms, pressing her head against his naked chest.

"Can you ever forgive me?" He whispered.

She sighed softly, wishing it could be that easy.

"I can only promise to try," she said. "I am still not sure if I love you or despise you."

"I cannot blame you for that. Had you not been wearing those heavy boots I would not have this chance to tell you how sorry I am. My fury would have taken me too far and how would I have lived with that when my deviant brother finally confessed for his own benefit?"

"His own benefit? How so?"

"He wanted my forgiveness in the hope of easing his way into heaven, to shorten his time in purgatory."

Philippa said nothing. Purgatory was something she had come to believe had no basis in truth, but now was not the time to discuss it.

"I would like to tell you it is in the past and no longer matters," she said, clasping him tighter around his bare waist. "The fact is I can forgive you losing control, I can even forgive what you did to me, but I cannot forgive you thinking I could ever betray you."

She was right; how could he have thought that? When he looked back to before he went away, to what they had, he knew she was right; he should have known.

"I have no excuse," he said softly. "Except I was so jealous and I had anticipated so much on my way back to you; I felt cheated. I wish there was something I could do to earn your forgiveness?" He asked. "Anything?"

She lifted her head and slid up to kiss his lips, then her mouth came down to his neck, brushed gently along his shoulders while her fingers played with his nipple and she began to breathe in short, gasping breaths.

"There might be," she whispered seductively between kisses. "I think you will have to keep trying to persuade me."

CHAPTER SEVEN

To wake and find his wife in his arms was a joy Lord Morton had never thought to have again, or even to want again. Her flesh, soft and naked against his own was nothing more than a memory which had haunted his dreams since the day he had walked out of this house, thinking never to return.

He had not thought when he decided to come here, when he had brought his child back to her mother, that the visit would ever include a night like last night, that she could ever want him again. He had done nothing to deserve it, so just how it had come about he could not say. Perhaps God was smiling on him for doing the right thing and reuniting his child with her mother.

Now all he wanted to do was stay here in this beautiful house, to lie in Philippa's arms and listen to the waves crashing against the rocks outside, the squawking of the seagulls, to watch Madeleine playing in the sea with her dog, laughing and happy. He did not want to go back to London, to the intrigue of King Henry's schemes to divorce his lawful wife, but he had to. He had sought leave to take time away for this very important family matter; if he did not return, the King would suspect him of devious plans against him. He had become more than a little suspicious of everyone of late, even turning against his best friends over this woman.

He wondered for the first time if perhaps the King did love the Lady Anne after all. He wondered if it were possible that he felt for her as Richard felt for Philippa. He would bring down the church for her if he had to, so perhaps the King was not simply besotted; perhaps he was really in love with the woman. Whatever his real feelings, if she also failed to give him a son, he would find some excuse to rid himself of her too. Richard could never see himself doing that.

Yesterday, Philippa suggested he might want to be free of her to find another wife, perhaps one who could give him a son. He shuddered at the idea, both of abandoning the love of his life for such a reason and of replacing her with someone else. She could have no more babies and the blame for that was his, he had done that to her. Was he now to desert her because of it?

This visit was intended to bring Madeleine home to her mother and to tell her how sorry he was, to face what he had done and hopefully correspond in polite, if not amicable terms with her in the future, nothing more. Since then he had learned that he did her a lot more harm than he had known and far from struggling to be on friendly terms, he had once more found himself in her arms, in her bed, inside her, needing her just as he always had. How he had lived all these years without her he could not guess, but he could not contemplate living without her again, not after this.

He would return to London and resign his post in the King's court. He would live quietly here with his wife and child, where he should have been all along - if she would have him, that is. She still had not forgiven him, may never forgive him, and may never know if she loved or loathed him. It would be a hard battle to win.

Her soft breathing tickled his chest and made his heart flutter with joy, made him stir once again. He pulled her close and kissed her, watched her eyes open.

"I did not feel you wake in the night," he remarked.

"I did not dream," she answered. "For the first time in years I did not dream. If you go away again, the dreams might come back."

"Do you want me to stay? I have been thinking about how I could do that, but only if you will have me. I cannot assume you will, even after last night."

Her eyes moved over his face, her emotions in turmoil again as she thought about his words.

"What did last night mean to you, Richard?" She asked.

"What do you mean?"

"I mean what did it mean to you? Was it to seal off the past, celebrate what we once had, or was it the beginning of a new future?"

"I think, I hope it can be a continuation of what we should never have lost, and yes, the beginning of a new future. But it is your choice, yours alone. I can ask nothing of you, I do not have the right."

She made no reply, but wrapped him in her arms and kissed him, a long and tender kiss which sent shivers through his body. She rolled away from him and stood up while he watched her beautiful body in the morning sunlight, her lovely curves and her shining flesh. How beautiful she was. Even with that horrible scar, she was still beautiful.

She pulled on a fresh shift and pushed her arms into a simple gown of the kind his daughter wore. He had forgotten how she always hated those heavy decorative clothes with their encrusted jewels and heavy skirts. She preferred to wear a simpler garment, one which would allow her more freedom to move as she painted her pictures. That was when he realised he had seen no new pictures. She had been sitting before her easel with her palette on the table beside it when they had arrived, but there was not a mark on the canvas.

"Have you no new paintings to show me?" He asked.

She looked at him in silence for a few moments as though trying to decide whether to reply.

"The last thing I painted was the beach, the one I sent for Madeleine to hang in her chamber. I have painted nothing since."

He sat up in surprise, suddenly afraid he had injured her hands during his blind rage, afraid of hearing he had caused another wound she had not mentioned.

"Why? Do you have some other injury you have told me nothing about?"

She was thoughtful for a moment as she brushed her hair and clipped it on top of her head. She placed a crown of flowers to encircle her head, and the effect made her look like some supernatural being, a fairy in the forest. She pulled her thick hair and the flowers forward to cover her scar before she replied.

"Only an injury of the spirit, Richard," she answered at last.

She walked to the bed and stood beside him, and he reached out his hand and took hers. He longed to take her in his arms but he felt suddenly afraid. Was last night an end for her, when he was thinking of it as a new beginning? He could not bear the idea.

"I must go and see Madeleine," she said, slipping away from him, "make sure she slept well. She will be unsettled in a strange house."

He watched her leave the chamber then began to dress. The conversation he would have to have with his wife would not be an easy one, but it had to be done. They had to know where they both stood, if their hopes for the future coincided. He could not assume that her need of him last night was proof that all was now well between them; that would be presumptuous in the extreme.

He went to the mirror which rested on the heavy cabinet where she had left her hairbrush. He picked it up and turned it over, studying the long, dark chestnut hairs which entwined themselves within the bristles. He opened the top drawer, hoping to find a comb, but instead he found a book. He was curious; although the printed book was slowly growing in popularity, it was an expensive item to obtain and still quite rare. He hardly expected to find such a thing in this remote part of the country.

He pulled it from the drawer and opened it, to reveal writings by the protestant reformer, Martin Luther. His heart felt that it would stop in his chest as he wondered what his wife was doing with such seditious and dangerous texts.

He opened the book, but had no time to begin reading before Philippa came back into the chamber. She stopped for only a moment, annoyed that he had pried into her cabinet and annoyed with herself for forgetting what was there. There were a lot more seditious writings but he had not found those, not yet at least.

"What is this?" He demanded.

Torn between memories of their recent lovemaking and a need to assert herself, her cheeks flushed and her anger flared.

"Have you somehow lost your ability to read, My Lord?" She demanded. "You can see well what it is. The writings of Martin Luther."

"What is it doing in my house?"

"It is mine," she said, feeling nervous now. "I have been studying it. He is a very perceptive man and he has some important ideas."

"Important and dangerous," he muttered.

He took a deep breath. He could see she was nervous, see she was unsure of his reaction to finding this book in her chamber, and he had no wish to make her nervous. She had never had to fear him, but since their last meeting things had changed and he did not want that. He did not want her to be afraid of him.

"Where did you get this idea?" He asked at last, trying to soften his tone.

Her eyes blazed with anger at his question, which perversely made him feel better. He much preferred her anger to her fear.

"Oh, of course!" She cried. "Someone must have put the ideas into my tiny little female head! Without your guidance, I have obviously been badly influenced. I could not possibly have thought to read it for myself."

"You know I have always had the utmost admiration and respect for your intellect, Philippa. That is not what I meant and you know it."

"Do I?"

"You must have heard of this man and his teachings from somewhere."

Yes, she had. She had listened to a preacher who was promptly dragged away and condemned for heresy before her eyes. She sighed, remembering the pity she had felt for that man, and her anger dissolved.

"There was a man preaching in the market square, giving out pamphlets," she said at last. "He was taken away by soldiers, rather brutally as it happens. It occurred to me that what he had to say must be important if he would risk his life to tell it."

His eyes met hers and his expression softened.

"You cannot have this here," he said soothingly, as though explaining to a child, as though reasoning with his daughter. He realised he sounded patronising and that would only anger her more.

"Ah, so you come back after seven years, not satisfied with telling me what I know, you must now tell me what to think and you will decide what I am and am not to read."

"I have never interfered with your reading or your study of any subject, you know that. But this is dangerous and I do not want you to endanger yourself for it. And it cannot be in the same house as my daughter."

She turned away and her mouth went down as tears began to gather. She thought of the weekly meetings of the little group to which she belonged, the little group of intelligent men and women who followed the teachings of Luther and compared them to the English Bible, to the teachings of Jesus Christ straight from his own lips, without the intervention of the established church, and in a language they could all understand. It was only the influence of Rome which declared Latin to be the language of God; it was the language of Rome, nothing more.

If Richard found out about them, God alone knew what he would do. He was not a devout Catholic by any means, but he believed in the religion and he believed in being on the side of the law. He would sign anything King Henry had to put in front of him to stay alive, but he would not go against the law.

"Ah, so now we have it," she finally replied. "You stole her away because you thought I would corrupt her with my lack of morals, now you think I will corrupt her with enlightened ideas. Do you imagine you are the only one concerned for her welfare?"

"Of course not."

"Have you read this?"

"No, I have not."

"You should. Did you know that the relics which the church charges people to see and to touch, are likely not the bones of saints at all, that the miraculous blood of Christ is likely from an animal? Do you know the lies they tell to enrich the Roman church?" She paused and drew a deep breath. "Did you know these rules were only thought up in the fourth century, the holy trinity, the eternal virgin? Now they are selling indulgences, telling people if they pay, they will spend less time in purgatory! Purgatory! Where does it even mention such a thing in the scriptures? It does not, that is why they do not want the Bible in English for everyone to read, because it makes a mockery of their dogma!"

"Philippa, please. You must have a care what you say."

"Why? You said yourself the King would break with Rome, set himself up as head of the church in England. Surely his next step will be to embrace these teachings."

"No. To get support for his break with Rome he is far more likely to be ever more zealous in enforcing church dogma. I cannot have this book and others like it under the same roof as Madeleine. She is an intelligent girl, but a very talkative one."

He watched her expression flame to anger again. He remembered well these sudden flashes of anger, but never before had they been directed at him. She bit her lip as she turned away, not wanting him to see the tears that gathered in her dark eyes.

"Well take her back to London, why not?" She shouted furiously. "Break her heart again, break mine. It is, after all, what you do best."

CHAPTER EIGHT

As Lord Morton left his wife's bedchamber he was torn in two directions. He did not expect to come home and find her reading heretical writings, but then what did he expect? If he had thought about her at all during those years, she was with Stephen, still sneaking meetings with his brother. Because he had not known the truth, it never occurred to him to wonder what she would be doing.

Now her angry words resounded in his ears and he knew that Madeleine would never forgive him if he took her away from her mother again.

He heard a bark as he came out on to the gallery to find Madeleine waiting there with Puddle, her pretty face furious, her hands bunched into fists on her hips. She had been listening, had heard every word. He cursed himself for a fool; this child of his was as independent as both her parents together. She would miss nothing, especially where it might affect her own future.

"Madeleine?" He said. "I did not know you were there."

"Are you going to take me back to London?" She demanded.

He swallowed an ache in his throat then moved quickly to stand before her, his hands gripping her shoulders through the thin summer gown she wore.

"I will do what is best for you, sweetheart," he said. "You must be sure of that."

"I do not want to go back to London," she declared. "I want to stay here with Mother."

"You should not be listening to other people's conversations," he admonished her.

"Conversations are not usually shouted and shrieked at the top of one's voice," she said stubbornly. "You promised me I could stay here. You promised Mother. I thought you were a man of your word."

"Madeleine, I am, you know that." He sighed heavily and released his grip on her, thinking how grown up she sounded, and how very much like her mother she was becoming. That same chestnut brown hair, that same stubborn nature, that same determined pout of her lips. He smiled, remembering the first time he had seen Philippa, when they had met to be wed. She was not much older than his daughter was now and that memory brought with it a reminder that he needed to conclude negotiations for a good match for Madeleine and he wanted her mother to be part of that. It was all getting very difficult.

"Well?" She demanded. "Am I to pack my boxes again? Am I to see my mother weeping again, like the last time you took me away from this house?"

He caught back a startled cry. She could not possibly remember that day, surely not.

"How much do you remember?" He asked hesitantly.

"Not very much. I remember hearing my mother scream though and I remember her sobbing as we rode away in the carriage."

"Nothing else?"

She shook her head and he breathed a sigh of relief.

"Please let me stay here, Father," she pleaded with a catch in her voice. "I will be leaving you both to marry soon enough. You will not take me back to London, will you?"

He smiled, still not sure what to do for the best.

"Not if I can avoid it," he said. "I have to discuss some things with your mother."

Philippa stood at the window with her arms folded, seething with quiet rage and staring out at the landscape. How dare he? Did he really believe she needed to be told that the books would have to go with Madeleine here? Did he really think she did not know that, that she would put her safety at risk? How dare he?

She did not turn when she heard the door opening and closing behind him. She felt certain she would hit him if he came closer and she did not want that. She was also unsure of how he would react if she did and that was a new and uncomfortable feeling.

"Forgive me," he said softly. "Philippa, I am sorry. I was just shocked to find that book here. Once again, I did not stop to think, to give you credit for knowing what to do. I never expected to find something like that here, never expected you to be reading such things."

She turned to face him at last, her anger still seething.

"What did you imagine I had been doing? Watching and waiting for you to pay me some attention?" He could not answer, could not tell her what he had really thought she was doing. "Did you even try to find Stephen, to take him to task, or were you satisfied with easing your temper on me?"

"I knew where he was," he began impulsively, then realised his mistake. "At least I thought I knew where he was."

She stared at him, unbelieving, her rage growing as she slowly realised what he meant.

"You thought he was here with me," she said at last, her arms dropping to her sides, her hands clenching into fists. "You believed I was happily living with my rapist and his bastard!"

"Philippa.........."

"You made no attempt to find him, to take revenge. You actually believed I had replaced you with him, replaced Madeleine with his son!"

He took a step toward her but she backed away until stopped by the window.

"The love of my life had turned on me, attacked me like some wild animal, and while I was mourning his loss and the loss of my child, you thought I was building a happy family with him?"

She almost choked on the words, she was so shocked, so angry.

"Philippa what can I say? I am so sorry."

He moved toward her once more, held out his arms but she slapped them away.

"Get out!" She cried. "Get out now! I swear if you stay here any longer I will find something heavy to hit you with. I will not be able to stop myself. Get out!"

When Richard went downstairs, Madeleine was waiting for him on the balcony, her arms folded and staring out to sea, her dog on the floor beside the wicker chair on which she sat. She looked at him defiantly and something inside made him laugh; she looked too small to be so angry.

"Well?" She demanded. "Am I to return to London?"

"No," he answered and was rewarded with her lovely smile. "But I must go and see if there is a young man of good birth who is good enough for my little girl."

She smiled timidly, then unfolded her arms.

"I read your letters," she said. He waited for her evaluation. "They are very fond letters. They make me think you fell in love with each other before you ever met."

He shrugged.

"Perhaps we did," he replied. "We seemed to have a lot in common. When we met to be wed I felt I had known her all my life. I believe she felt the same about me. I would very much like to achieve that for you."

"Why do you not still love each other?" She asked.

Her question gave him pause. *Why indeed? Because your father is a bloody fool,* he wanted to say. *Because he failed to recognise what a priceless gem he had captured.*

"I think we do still love each other, Madeleine. I know I still love her, but there was a terrible misunderstanding which hangs between us and likely always will. It is not easy to turn back and heal a breach that wide. When we find someone for you, you can write, find out if he is the sort of person you might fall in love with."

"And if he is not?" She asked.

"Then we will think again. You will not be forced into marriage with anyone, trust me on that. I would never allow it and your mother would never forgive me."

He leaned forward and kissed her forehead affectionately while she smiled.

"I am going to move out of the nursery this afternoon," she told him, "if that meets with your approval. Alice says I am too old to sleep in the nursery. I thought you might allow me that big chamber which looks out over the sea, the one at the other end of the house from you and mother."

You and mother.

She was assuming they would share a bed, when he had not yet had an answer as to whether his wife wanted him there at all. Considering their latest conversation, he somehow doubted it. He wondered how he could have made such a mess of everything, even of this second chance she seemed likely to allow. He thought about last night, the passion they had shared. It was almost as though they had never parted and now he had ruined it again.

Why had he made such a fuss about the book? He knew she would allow nothing to hurt Madeleine. He did not want to hurt his daughter again, or elicit more awkward questions.

"You choose whichever one you want," he said. "Go now. I have more things to talk with your mother about."

He watched her go, the dog trotting along behind her, then he went to his wife's bedchamber to see if he could repair the latest damage.

She was sorting through her cabinet, piling papers and scrolls on top as well as another book, this one hand written and obviously valuable. She turned and glared at him angrily.

"This is everything, My Lord," she told him. "I will return them all to my friend this afternoon. I have sent a message for her to meet me and she will make certain they do not fall into the wrong hands."

She shuffled all the documents into a pile and turned to face him defiantly.

"Are there any more orders, any more rules you wish to impose on me before you agree to my having the care of my own child?" She demanded.

He shook his head, feeling ashamed all over again.

"I am growing weary of apologising, Philippa, but once again, I am sorry. I have been solely responsible for Madeleine's wellbeing for a long time; I suppose I just assumed responsibility. Forgive me."

"That was your own doing," she answered bitterly.

But his words dispelled a little of her anger and she looked up at him, hoping he could not see the distress he had caused this time. Something had to be done; he could not stay here and make her angry enough to strike out because of his distrust. She needed to think, needed him out of her sight.

"My Lord," she said, "would you do me the favour of removing yourself from my presence. I need to think and to rest. I can do neither with you here. I am sure Madeleine will appreciate your company."

He left her, as she requested, and went to the balcony to watch his daughter running along the sand, throwing a ball for her dog. She would not venture into the sea unless someone was with her, so he knew she was safe and he did not feel in the mood to talk to her. He had so much to think about, so many wrongs for which to make amends. He sat on the wicker chair where he had found his wife when he first arrived, and pondered his future.

When he decided to come here he had not expected any sort of reconciliation and despite the love they had shared last night, nothing had really changed. When he left Stephen to draw his last breath in the care of the monks of Blackfriars, it never occurred to him to change his assumption about Philippa's activities, except a fleeting idea that she might have another man in her life, an idea he had dismissed as ludicrous.

Now he realised how betrayed she must feel, to know he had not only beaten and abandoned her, but believed her to be living quite happily with his brother, a man Alice told him she had never liked, never trusted, a man who had violated her, humiliated her and destroyed that special bond she always had with her husband. The love of her life she had called him and look how he had shown his appreciation, look how he had valued that most precious of gifts.

As he watched, Puddle came tearing up the beach towards him, his paws covered in wet sand, closely followed by Madeleine. Richard was too despondent to even get out of the dog's way before he put his huge, wet, sandy paws on his legs, soaking his breeches as he licked his face enthusiastically.

"Puddle!" Madeleine cried out, too late to call him off. "I am sorry, Father."

"No matter," he replied with a smile. "I thought you were busy moving into that grown up bedchamber."

She looked sheepish for a moment before she replied.

"I wanted to wait until I was sure you would allow me to stay," she answered.

"Of course you will stay," he said. "I promised you and I promised your mother. I do not break my promises. Go, make it special, make it yours."

She kissed his cheek and hurried away while he sat some more and watched the waves, knowing he would likely have to give all this up again and return to London. At last he got to his feet; his clothes were wet and covered in sand and he would have to go and change them, make another attempt to change his wife's mood.

She was lying on the bed in her shift when he opened the door, and on the floor beside her were the documents and books she had earlier taken from her cabinet. He glanced down at them, saw the title page where the book had fallen open, then his eyes moved back to Philippa.

"Are you ill, My Lady?" He asked.

"No," she answered, "only hot. I wanted to rest before I took these back to my friend. I have been lying here wondering what to tell her."

He thought it best to make no suggestions, to let her decide for herself. His input would likely be unwelcome and he had no wish to quarrel again.

His eyes moved over her where she lay, watched the outline of her body, naked beneath the thin cotton shift, and he felt that passionate stirring which he could neither control nor hide. He sat on the bed beside her and leaned forward to kiss her, to drink in her lips and taste her beauty. His hand cupped her breast, he stroked the bottom of her stomach, traced the curves of her body with his fingers. She made no objection, only lay still, her breath coming in little panting murmurs, and watched him until his hand moved to settle inside her thigh and he leaned forward and kissed her again.

"Do you still love me?" He asked.

"I will always love you," she answered softly, "but that does not keep me from hating you."

He stood and removed his clothes, laid down beside her and untied the ribbons of her shift so that it slipped down her shoulders, releasing her breasts to his mouth and his hands. His lips moved over her from her neck, along her shoulders and down, down to rest between her thighs.

Oh god! How he wanted her, had never stopped wanting her. He had wanted her all these years but each time he felt that need, he had snuffed it out with an image of her with his brother, of the little flutter from an unborn child that he had not put there.

He felt her lips on his nipple, felt her tongue on his chest, felt the warm panting breath coming from her and he pulled her close against him, felt her hands urgently caressing his back and shoulders and laid her on her back to fill her with his hardness, the little moans and cries which escaped her adding to his desire. He wanted to bury himself inside her and stay there forever and he cursed himself for all the years he had thrown away, all the years he had let Stephen steal from them.

For the next hour they dozed in each other's arms and felt the warmth pass between them. He wanted to stay here in Cornwall with her, he wanted that so much, but still he had not had that answer, and still he was afraid to ask the question.

Now he watched her as she rolled off the bed and reached for her shift. He put out his hand and trailed his fingers down her back, felt her shiver and stretch her shoulders toward him. She turned and smiled, then stood and pulled on her simple velvet petticoat, her kirtle and sat before the mirror to place her headdress on her head, pulling the flowers around her cheeks to cover the blemish. He felt ashamed each time he watched her cover that scar, whether with her silk shawl or her headdress of flowers, or anything else and he shuddered with disgust at himself.

She returned to the bed and gathered up the scrolls and the book.

"Wait," he said, pushing away the covers and preparing to sit up. "I will come with you."

"Why?" He made no reply, but began to dress. "You want to be sure they get there," she said with a note of accusation. "You do not trust me to take them?"

She could scarcely believe it. After the love they had shared, after dropping her guard and allowing herself to resume that intimacy which she had so loved, he was now going to prove he still did not trust her.

"So all your supposed regrets meant nothing then?" She demanded.

Still he did not argue, just turned and looked at her. He had no wish to admit she was right, but she was. He wanted to make quite sure the heretical writings left his house for good.

"How dare you?" She cried. "How dare you accuse me of lying to you, of trying to deceive you? Do you think I want to risk Madeleine finding these and reading them, talking about them? Do you think I want to risk her safety?"

"I know you would not but..."

"Never mind," she interrupted him then threw the documents down onto the bed and her mouth went down. "I will wait for you. If you do not see them leave the house for yourself, who knows but you might take my child from me again."

He took one long stride to stand before her, feeling hurt by her words and hurt that he had, once again, brought her to tears. Why did he do that, when it was the very last thing he wanted? He put his arms around her and held her close, but she made no response, only stood with her arms at her sides.

"You know I will not do that," he assured her.

"I know nothing! Let go of me, please. We will get this errand done then you can begin your journey back to London."

"Is that what you want?"

"Yes, it is. If you cannot trust me to keep Madeleine safe, and I cannot trust you not to take her away from me again, what have we left?"

Philippa waited in the ruin of the little arbour in the woods where she had asked her friend to meet her. As she waited, she read over the forbidden text which had been the cause of the arguments, trying to memorise them, as it was unlikely she would have a chance to read them again.

A rustle among the trees made her look up.

"Selena," she greeted the other woman, as she got to her feet, putting the books and documents down on the marble seat where she had been sitting. She moved towards her and took both her hands in her own. "Thank you for coming so soon."

"You cancelled the meeting," Selena said. "We were worried. We held it at my house after all, but we did not know what was happening. Is all well with you?"

Philippa released her hands and turned to pick up the heavy books, which she wrapped carefully in a piece of muslin cloth she had brought with her. She wanted no one to see what they were as Selena would have to carry them through the village to her home.

As she quickly wrapped them, she looked around nervously, expecting Richard to be watching from a hiding place among the trees. After their latest argument he assured her he did trust her and he had no need to accompany her, but she did not believe him. After the way he had shown his distrust of her, she saw no reason to believe him.

She fully expected him to be watching and listening to every word.

"I want you to take these," she told her friend. "They are the only copies we have and I do not want them to fall into the wrong hands."

"What do you mean?"

Philippa passed the documents and books to her friend then sighed softly.

"There will be no more meetings for me," she said.

"What? You are our best teacher." Her eyes were wide as she stared at her friend in alarm. "Have you been discovered?"

"In a way, yes," she replied. "But we have nothing to fear; we will not be betrayed." She paused and took a deep breath. "I have my daughter back."

Selena gave her a puzzled frown and shook her head, her eyes narrowing.

"I knew nothing of a daughter."

No, she would know nothing. Philippa had never mentioned her child to her new friends, partly because she wanted no one to know about Madeleine, but also because she could never bear to speak of her, not to anyone, not even to Alice.

"She is twelve years old," she explained. "My husband took her away, seven years ago. Now he has brought her back and I cannot risk losing her again."

Selena leaned back against a tree trunk, her expression one of curiosity.

"I am sorry, Philippa," she said. "I did not even know you were married and now you tell me you have a husband and child. I always mistook you for a widow."

Selena likely thought their visits to this little arbour to be trespassing.

"It is a long and complicated story," Philippa replied, "and one I have no wish to talk about."

Selena stared at her and her eyes moved to the mark on her cheek; she frowned suspiciously and Philippa was afraid she had guessed where that scar had come from, but she said nothing about it. She wondered what Selena was thinking, how it would look to her. She had been told her friend had not seen her husband or child in years, she bore an ugly blemish on her face; of course it must be fairly apparent where it had come from.

"I still do not understand," Selena persisted. "Surely you will want to teach her."

Conscious that Richard was likely to be listening to every word she wanted to be certain he heard her reject the idea and she suddenly felt unsure of her friend, suspicious even. She had never felt like that before, but now she did not feel she could trust her. It seemed as though she disapproved and there was a little fanatical gleam in her eye which made Philippa uneasy.

"I will not put her in danger," she replied firmly. "I must choose between my daughter and our studies or I could lose her again. There can be no choice. I will not give him an excuse to take her from me a second time." She took her friend's hands again. "You do understand?"

She hoped he was listening, hoped he could hear the bitterness in her voice, hear that she suspected him of looking for reasons to take Madeleine away again. It would do him good to know he had no right to simply step back into her life and take it over.

Selena made no reply but she looked over Philippa's shoulder and her eyes narrowed. Philippa turned to see her husband standing and observing the scene, just as she suspected. She released her friend's hands.

"Richard," she greeted him. "This is Mistress Wright, my friend." She turned to the other woman. "Selena, may I present my husband, the Earl of Morton."

Selena gave her a surprised glance, then curtsied.

"My Lord," she murmured.

"Mistress," he replied with a bow. "If I am interrupting I can talk to my wife later."

"No," Philippa replied hastily, her eyes moving to the heavy books in Selena's arms. "Selena was about to leave."

The two women glanced at each other then Selena turned and hurried away, her arms wrapped around the parcel clutched to her chest, while Philippa turned back to her husband accusingly.

"I knew you would follow me," she said angrily. "All your talk about trusting me meant nothing did it?"

It was obvious to her that he too was angry, although she could not fathom why. He was the one who was following her, spying on her. She had done as he asked, or rather ordered; she had returned the books and told her friend she would break from the group. What more did he want?

"Meetings?" He said. "In my house?"

Ah, so that was it.

"I thought it was my house?" She replied, recalling his words of the night before.

"It is your sanctuary if you want it as such," he answered with an angry note. "But it is my house and I do not want meetings of heretics taking place inside it."

"Since you were listening, you must have heard me tell Selena that there will be no more meetings for me. Does that not satisfy you?"

"Providing you give me your word," he answered. "I do not want to take Madeleine away again, and I do want you to be safe. Do you promise me?"

She looked up at him and her heart began to beat rapidly. She was angry with him for forcing a promise, when he should have known that nothing would make her put Madeleine's safety at risk. But her treacherous memory could feel his fingers stroking her skin, could feel his lips on her breasts and inside her thighs, could show her every blissful detail of their recent times together and make her long for more.

She turned away from him, afraid to face those feelings. Delighted as she was to have Madeleine back, she began to wish he had stayed away. Their passion was as alluring as it had ever been and that passion was irresistible, but it seemed that was all they had now. They really did have very little left on which to build a future.

"Do you..." he began hesitantly, "do you have any more heretical writings you want to return to your friends?"

She did not answer him. A little voice inside her head was telling her he had no right to come back here and tell her what to read, while another voice told her he had every right, she was still his wife. She was confused about which one to follow.

"No," she finally replied. "They have all gone."

She moved away from him and went back to the house. He was doing it again, misjudging her when he should have known better. That made her angry, very angry.

She was so confused. Only a few days ago she was beginning another lonely day during which she would watch the waves, go for a walk, perhaps see her friends. Then he had arrived and put her in a state of bewilderment. She had no idea what to do, which way to turn and she cursed herself for inviting him into her bed. The decision would be much easier had she kept her distance, but remembering how she had felt when she first saw him, how she still felt, it might have been an impossible task.

She made her way to the nursery floor; there was only one person she would trust with intimate secrets such as these.

Alice sat beside the window looking down at the beach, at the waves crashing against the rocks, at Lord Morton strolling along the sand, alone. She turned when she heard the door open.

"May I talk to you?" Philippa asked.

"Of course, My Lady," Alice replied. "That is what I am here for. You are troubled, I can see."

Philippa came further into the room and sat down beside the old nurse, glancing out of the window at her husband on the beach below.

"I am so confused, Alice," she said. "I wish I knew what to do. He wants us to try again, he wants to give up his post at court and stay here."

The old nurse studied her for a few moments, her eyes filled with compassion. She knew that Alice was unforgiving when it came to Richard and his brother, despite the latter's death, and she thought that might make her advise against a reconciliation, which would not help Philippa at all. She wanted an unbiased opinion and now she wondered if she had come to the wrong person for it.

But where else to go? The village priest would tell her he was her husband and her duty lie with him. If he wanted to come back, she had no right to question it according to the church, so she would certainly not find neutral advice in that direction. She would also have to explain to him what the rift was about in the first place, and that was something she would never do. Besides, she had little time for catholic priests. What could a celibate priest tell her about the love between a man and a woman? Absolutely nothing.

"Is that what you want?" Alice asked at last.

Philippa glanced at her hands where they sat in her lap, twisting around each other.

"That is the problem," she said without looking up. "Part of me wants that more than anything, but the other part of me wants to kill him. Does that sound ridiculous?"

Alice reached out and gently moved the hair away from her face.

"After what he did to you?" She replied. "No, it does not sound ridiculous."

Philippa touched her face where Alice's fingers had rested.

"This is nothing," she said. "It is the time afterwards I am struggling with. Do you know what he thought? He thought I was living here quite happily with Stephen! How dare he? How do I get over that?"

Alice took her hand and gently held on to it.

"I should have told him," Philippa said. "If I had told him how I felt about Stephen, he might have known straight away."

"But you kept that to yourself for Richard's sake, because you did not want to distress him."

Philippa nodded.

"My Lady," Alice said soothingly, "you are still in love with him, that is obvious to me, but can you forgive him?"

"That is what I am not sure of."

"You are still young, both of you. You should not live the rest of your lives apart and miserable, missing each other. Think of how it will be when Madeleine is wed and gone from here."

"Will you forgive him, Alice?" Philippa asked, looking up into the nurse's face.

She slowly shook her head.

"I can try, for your sake," she said, "but I loved both those boys like they were my own and I cannot forget the way they behaved, either of them. I wish you had told me the truth of it. I could see how melancholy you were, but I thought it was missing Richard, that all would be well when he returned. I knew nothing; I did not even know you were with child."

"Neither did Stephen," Philippa answered. "I wanted no one to know until I had to tell Richard. That was my plan, that if he came home after the birth, I would never have to tell him at all, he would never have to be hurt. That is why I wanted no one to know."

"So you went through all the worry and the sickness alone? Just to keep him from being hurt?" Alice held tighter to her hand. "And I suppose you would have given birth alone, sneaked off to the barn to have a child in secret, risked your life to protect a man who does not deserve you." Alice's voice had risen as she spoke; now she stopped to bring it under control. She shook her head again. "No," she said, "I do not think I can forgive him. But that does not mean you should not. You are tied together and you still love each other. It would be a tragic waste of two lives for you to spend them apart. And think how happy Madeleine will be."

Philippa glanced once more at the beach below, saw Richard returning slowly to the house. She hesitated before telling Alice more.

"We have thrice made love since he came home," she said. She looked up at the old nurse with wide, doubtful eyes. "Was that wrong?"

"Did it feel wrong?"

"No. God, no! Nothing could have felt more right."

"He is your husband," Alice said. "Of course it is not wrong. And if you can still enjoy each other, you have to try to move forward."

She took a deep, decisive breath. Alice's words were like an invitation to happiness.

"Yes, Alice. You are right, as always. Thank you. I will tell him to resign his post in London and come home. We will try to make it work, even if we never have back what we once had."

As she made her way downstairs, her thoughts were still racing. *What we once had.* That was the memory they needed to get past. Before Stephen there had been no one else for either of them.

She sat on the bottom stair, wanting to finish the recollection before she had to talk to anyone and her memory took her back to that night.

She woke to realise it was Stephen who was in her bed, who was touching her, kissing her, now she remembered how different it was to Richard. She felt nauseous, even before he forced himself inside her; she always welcomed her husband into her body. She had never known anything else and that made it somehow even worse, that some invader was forcing his way into that special place, that special privilege, and there was nothing she could do to stop it.

She had avoided thinking about it since it happened and now she wished she had left it alone.

CHAPTER NINE

He left that afternoon to begin the long journey back to London, still not sure if he was returning to resign his post with the King or to move back to his lonely London house.

He kissed Madeleine goodbye in her new bedchamber which she was excitedly arranging, helping herself to bits of furniture and ornaments from the rest of the house as well as from the nursery. She carefully hung some portraits her mother had painted when Madeleine was just a baby, portraits of her laughing and clapping her hands.

"Mother said I could keep them in here," she told him excitedly. "Are they not beautiful?" She stopped talking and stood back to admire the affect, her hands behind her back as she said proudly: "My mother is very clever."

Yes, she certainly was clever, gifted with a unique talent and he could only pray she would paint again, now she at least had her daughter back, even if she did not want him. He would have to learn to live with that, although it would be one of the hardest things he had ever had to do. It would have been easier had he not shared her bed, had he not made love to her on three wonderful occasions since he came here, had he not felt her fingers gently playing around his nipple, had not felt her tongue on his groin, had not felt her passionate lips on his.

He gave a deep sigh and shook his head. There might still be a chance for them; he decided to swallow his pride and try one more time.

He met his wife beside the waiting carriage and caught her up in his arms, kissed her deeply and her shiver of delight gave him hope.

"I want to return to London and resign my post at court. I want to tell the King I am going home to my wife and my daughter." He paused and held her close again. "But I will wait for word from you. Please write, Philippa, if only to tell me to stay away. I want to hear how Madeleine is and I want to know you are safe. I want to discuss Madeleine's marriage with you."

"Do you have someone in mind?"

"I have been negotiating with the Earl of Loughridge. He has a son the same age as Madeleine so a marriage would have to wait another two years, but that will suit us both I should think. I will do nothing without your agreement."

"Thank you." She held him close once more, then pushed him away. "Have a safe journey, My Lord," she said.

"So I am to leave without an answer?"

"I am sorry, Richard. I need more time to consider, to think clearly without the distraction of your presence. Please."

He pulled her close and held her against him once more.

"Whatever you want," he said.

She watched the carriage until it was out of sight, still torn in two directions, still longing to feel his flesh touching hers while wanting to tear him apart at the same time. Despite what she had told Alice, she wanted more time to think about it.

She was hurt that he had not trusted her to remove the writings from the house and she was hurt that he would take her child away again if she did not comply with his wishes.

That was not the sort of marriage they had had before Stephen. Then they had trusted each other with anything and everything, they could talk about their innermost fears and feelings without fear of reproach. He had never expected obedience from her; he had always expected her to speak her thoughts, to discuss her wants and needs with him. It seemed that had all changed and she was unsure if she could live with him now, although she wanted to desperately. If only London were not such a very long way away, they would be able to move forward gradually, see each other without that final step.

She almost wished he would exercise his right to return to his wife whether she liked it or not. As her husband, there was nothing she could do to stop him; it was a concession and a sign of respect that he was giving her leave to decide.

A little cough from behind her made her turn and smile at her maidservant where she stood holding a rolled up piece of parchment. It bore Selena's handwriting and she was thankful that this servant could not read. Most of them could not, which made it safe to send messages in their hands.

"My Lady," she said, giving a brief curtsey.

She held out the letter and stepped away once it was safely in Her Ladyship's hands. Philippa glanced quickly about before breaking the seal and taking the letter to the little arbour where she was accustomed to meeting her friend. It was deep inside the woods, in ruins now from disuse, and mostly home to many species of wildlife. She sat on the little marble stool and unrolled the letter, hoping it was not an invitation to another meeting when she had been clear that there would be no more for her. She let her eyes skim over it quickly before she moved deeper into the woods to a small hut where her friend was asking her to meet.

It was a tiny, round hut, not big enough to be called a cottage or a dwelling of any kind, but it had a thatched roof and a wooden door, one window opening with dilapidated wooden shutters.

She was puzzled, wondering what on earth she wanted and just why they were not meeting in their usual place. She did not have to wait long to learn the answer. As she approached the hut the door opened and Selena stood on the threshold, beckoning her inside.

Philippa wished she had not asked to see her. Although Richard had gone, although she saw him leave with her own eyes, she still had the uncomfortable feeling that he knew she was meeting Selena and would use the knowledge to distrust her again.

She was anxious to get this meeting over and done with, to return to the house before she was seen.

"What is wrong?" She asked at once, making her way inside. She waited while Selena closed the door and secured it, then turned to face her.

"They have been arrested," she said.

"What? All of them? How?"

"You tell me."

Her friend's tone was angry and resentful, her words filled with suspicion. Philippa's eyes grew round and she sank down on to the bench.

"What are you saying?"

"It is something of a coincidence, I think, that your husband arrives, makes you give up your studies, has no sooner left and they are all arrested?" Philippa interrupted with a finger to her own lips in an effort to make her control her voice which was rising rapidly; she could not afford for them to be overheard. "I returned from the village to see the soldiers leaving my father's house; they had gathered the entire group. I was the only one who escaped and that by sheer chance."

"Selena," Philippa said miserably, "you surely do not think that Richard would betray us."

"Why not? He made quite sure no evidence remained against you."

"No," Philippa was shaking her head violently, desperately trying to find some other explanation. "What will happen to them?"

"The men will burn, I imagine. The women will hang if they are lucky."

Philippa caught her breath as she felt her world collapsing once again. Of course he would know what their fate would be, and for that reason alone she could not accept his guilt.

"Selena, I promise you," Philippa said, reaching out her hand and pulling her friend to sit beside her. "Richard would never do this."

Selena pushed the flowers away from Philippa's cheek, revealing the folded flesh which marred her face.

"Just as he would never do that," she demanded angrily.

Philippa quickly pulled the flowers forward to hide the blemish, her face flushed with embarrassment.

"How did you know?" She asked, thinking it rather pointless to deny it now.

"I saw the ring he wears," she replied. "It was not hard to guess."

Philippa kept her eyes on her clasped hands, afraid to think about what this new turn of events meant to her hopes for the future. His wish to try again had been so intense, his pleas so genuine, surely he would not risk the possibility of a future for them? But Selena was right: it was too much of a coincidence for this to happen now. For years the group had met in secret without a hint of discovery, then Richard came home and found the books. *I want to know that you are safe.* That is what he had said and what else could he have meant but that he was expecting trouble? It had to be him, there was no other explanation and she felt so disappointed she could have cried.

Just when she had almost made up her mind to take him back, to give them another chance, everything was being snatched away again.

"You must stay here," Philippa told her. "I will bring some bedding and food. I would happily have you stay in the house, but it is likely soldiers are searching for you and I cannot put Madeleine at risk."

"Of course," Selena replied. "I would expect nothing else."

She reached out again and ran the back of her fingers delicately along the scar, feeling its shape, its folds.

"If you want to forgive him for that," she said, "that is your choice. But please do not tell me you can forgive him the deaths of all our friends."

Philippa returned to the house to gather blankets and prepare a basket of food to take to her friend while the kitchens were quiet. She would hide them away until after dark; she could not afford to be discovered.

She had not felt this miserable since that awful day when he attacked her, when he had taken away her child. She thought he could do nothing more to her, but now she saw she was wrong. She looked out to see Madeleine playing on the beach with Puddle under the watchful gaze of a manservant, just far enough away from the house to be safe but not close enough to hear. Philippa knew she was about to break down again and she had no desire for Madeleine to bear witness to it.

She sat beside the empty hearth and caught her breath as the tears began to form. She had cried too much since Richard left her, but it seemed to her she had cried more these few days since he decided to return. Her memory was showing her his tender lovemaking, his passionate kisses, the bliss of his hardness inside her, none of which she would ever feel again. Selena was right; she could forgive the brutality he had inflicted on her in a blind rage, but she could not forgive the betrayal of all her friends.

"My Lady?" Alice's voice came from the doorway, then she hurried forward and sat beside her, gathering her into her arms.

Alice was more than a servant; she was part of the family, a big part of the family, and she could do and say whatever she liked to all of them, even to Philippa who she had known since her marriage, not since birth like Richard and his brother. It had been Alice who made Stephen leave that day. He returned once Richard had gone, expecting to carry on living in the house as though nothing had happened. He had gone to Philippa and spoken to her as though it was her fault.

"You know," he said, "if you had not told my brother what happened between us, he would never have known. I do not understand why you could not keep your mouth shut."

"Nothing happened between us, Stephen!" She shouted at him. "You raped me, that is what happened. Was I to keep that from my husband, from the man I love? I told no one, all this time, just waiting for Richard to be safe before I broke the news about what a depraved deviant his brother is."

"Oh, come now, Philippa," he said, looking offended. "That's a bit harsh. It was only once."

"Because I locked you out!"

As she spoke she held a bloody cloth to her face, but he did not seem to even notice. Neither did he notice her flinch and double up with pain, as that is the moment the miscarriage started.

"Well, yes," he mumbled, "I am sorry. I misinterpreted, I admit. But you should not have told him."

Alice came in then; she had overheard. She stood in the doorway and her eyes moved from Philippa to Stephen. Philippa gulped in an effort to stop the pain but all Alice noticed was the blood which continued to soak the cloth.

"He raped you?" She demanded. "Why in God's name did you not tell me?"

Philippa looked up at her from her position on the bed.

"I did not want you to risk Richard's safety by writing to him," she answered. "I thought I would have time to explain when he came home."

"Stephen," Alice turned angry eyes on him. "How could you? Did I raise you to abuse women? Did I?" She stepped forward and slapped his face and he jumped back, clutching his cheek in his hand.

"It was a misunderstanding, Alice, that was all!"

"No, it was you not wanting to listen, as always. You will leave this house at once and never return. If Richard knew what you had done he would kill you." She knelt before Philippa and took her quivering shoulders in her hands. "Why did you not tell him, Philippa?" She said. "Why let him think the worst?"

"I did tell him," she answered miserably. "He did not believe me."

"He will get over it," Stephen muttered.

"Please make him leave, Alice, please."

She did. She sent a servant to pack his things and told him again never to return. When she came back Philippa was barely conscious and a flow of red was blossoming across her skirt.

Philippa thought it likely that Alice blamed herself for the way both men had behaved, as she was the one who had raised them from birth, but Richard was a good man, he was always a good man. It was blind rage that made him lose control, a human reaction to a terrible situation, and she could forgive that. But there was no rage to excuse his betrayal of her friends.

"What is wrong, My Lady?" Alice asked gently. "Are you this distraught that His Lordship has gone back to London?"

Philippa shook her head as she sat up, trying desperately to control her emotions but having little success.

"He has betrayed them," she answered, between sobs. "My friends. They have all been arrested! How could he? They are no threat to anyone; they are ordinary, simple folk whose only wish was to learn more and use the reasoning powers God gave them. They are not rebels or violent activists. Why would he do that?"

She felt Alice's body stiffen, felt the shaking of her head.

"Why are you sure it was Richard?" She asked.

"Who else? We have met unmolested for years, we have read our books and kept our counsel, have discussed the writings without interference from anyone. Then he came back and found my books. Now they will all die, so what else am I to think?"

"But surely it is a coincidence?"

"He made me return all the books and writings to Selena, he even insisted on coming with me. Was that so he could discover who she was? He made certain nothing remained here, nothing to incriminate me." She stared at Alice as a sudden alarming thought came to her. "If any one of them thinks it was me who betrayed them, they might incriminate me. Oh, Alice, do you think that is what he wants?"

"What? No of course not! Why would he?"

"Perhaps so he can have Madeleine back or...Oh, I do not know!"

"If that were the case he had no need to bring her here at all. You are letting your imagination run away with you."

Philippa gripped Alice's hands tightly. She had no control over the tears which flowed down her hot cheeks, soaking into her neck, reminding her sharply of the blood that had soaked into her neck. Alice took out a cloth and wiped her face, then put her arm around her and drew her head down onto her shoulder.

"Tell me he could not do this," Philippa murmured. "Please Alice; tell me he is incapable of doing this. It is not even as though he were a devout Catholic. Please, tell me I am wrong."

Alice made no reply. There was a time when she could have given that assurance without hesitation, but one look at her mistress's cheek told her she could no longer be sure.

"I would love to tell you what you want to hear," she said. "But I no longer know what he could or could not do. You have no idea how much I would give to be able to give you the assurance you seek, but I cannot, not any more."

"Mother?" Her daughter's breathless voice came from the doorway. "Why are you crying?"

Both women studied the girl's soaking frock and hair, the wet sand which clung to her hem and to the dog, her eyes sparkling with excitement.

"I am sad, Madeleine," she answered with effort, "because your father has gone back to London."

Madeleine smiled, a little knowing smile which told them both she was pleased. She would lie if she had to; she wanted nothing to spoil that joy.

She waited to hear her daughter's footsteps running up the stairs, hear the dog's paws trotting along beside her, then she turned back to Alice and rested her head against her bosom.

"We were going to have a fresh start," she whispered mournfully. "We were going to try to repair the damage. I love him so much; I thought we had a chance. Why did he do this? Why did he have to spoil it, after everything he said?"

CHAPTER TEN

Back in his London house, Lord Morton keenly felt the emptiness of the building without Madeleine, without the dog pacing around after her. When he left London to reunite her with her mother, he had not thought for one moment there was any chance of a reconciliation between himself and his wife; he was only afraid of how he would react to seeing her again, whether his memory would let him forget the anger and hatred he always felt. He knew the London house would be a lonely place to return to, but it was worse than he had thought, now he had savoured the enchantment of his wife's body again, now he had sat on the balcony and watched the waves, heard them crashing against the rocks in the night, held tight to Philippa to shut out the noise from the sea.

He had angered her before he left and he wished it had not happened. He was not sure why it happened, why he felt the need to oversee the return of the heretical writings to her friends. It was not through lack of trust, as she had assumed, it was for his own peace of mind. He was so concerned for the safety of his wife and his daughter. And he felt keenly that he would never tell her what to read and what not to read, but he had to think of Madeleine. Was that so very wrong? He prayed she would write, she would miss him and want him back with her. That is all he wanted now.

While he waited, he wrote letters to the Earl of Loughridge to continue negotiations for a marriage between his son and Madeleine. It was a great responsibility and one he wanted very much to share with his wife; he did not want the decision to be his alone lest he make the wrong one. His daughter's happiness was paramount.

The first glimpse of Philippa's handwriting on a letter set his heart racing. He hesitated to break the seal, afraid of what she had written. One line stood out, just one, and he felt defeated and lost.

I could have forgiven you for the past, for Madeleine, but I cannot forgive this latest betrayal, Richard. It is just too much. Please stay away.

He could only assume she meant his distrust, his insistence on overseeing the return of the heretical writings to her friend. He would not have called it a betrayal himself, but she obviously felt that it was, and it was too much? After what he had done to her, beating her, leaving her barren, scarring her and taking her child away...he could not believe she could forgive all that but find his wanting to be sure of her safety the final straw. Perhaps it was simply the very last thing, one more thing for which she had to search her heart to forgive and it was just too much.

He moved to the writing bureau and was about to sit and reply to her letter, when a manservant entered the room. He bowed to his master as he looked up, but had no chance to speak before Olivia swept into the room behind him, a dazzling smile pasted onto her face as though she had prepared it in advance, and she probably had.

"Richard!" She cried and ran to him, took his hands. "I am so relieved to have you home. I was worried."

He dismissed the servant with a nod of his head then turned to her.

"What are you doing here, My Lady? I told you I had no wish to see you again. Did you not understand?"

"I know you did but I realised when I learned where you had gone, that you were preoccupied with other things and could not have meant it."

"And how did you learn where I had gone?" He demanded. "You must have come here, asking questions, or even worse enquired at court. I thought I made it quite clear I do not approve of your making enquiries about me."

"I was concerned," she said, "you going off to Cornwall, to visit your wife. I was afraid she might capture you under her spell again."

His temper flared and he felt the need to strike out, but he controlled his anger with great difficulty.

"What business is that of yours?"

"Perhaps none," she answered quietly. "But I do not want to see you hurt again. It has been a long time since you caught her in adultery. Do you imagine she has slept alone all these years?"

His hands clenched into fists and he could feel the fury rising, almost as fierce as seven years ago. He had tried hard never to lose his temper again, but this woman was pushing him too far. When he remembered the few nights he had so recently spent in his wife's arms, when he recalled the awful mistakes which had caused them to part, the damage he had done her and the love his wife still had for him, he could not keep his temper while this whore invaded his home once again and insulted the best woman who ever lived! He would tolerate no more of it.

"I tell you what she has been doing," he said, his voice rising to a shout. "She has been finding different styles to hide a hideous scar on her face, a scar which I put there, a scar made by this!" He clenched his fist and held his ring close to her face. "Would you like one to match?"

It took all his willpower not to carry out his threat, then he pulled off the ring and threw it across the room, where it bounced off the wall and ricocheted to hit the back of her head.

"Now get out!" He yelled. "If you ever come to my house again, you will not leave it alive."

She ran, her hand to her mouth to stave off a scream, and fled to the door. He heard it slam, heard her carriage move off, and sank down in his chair to calm his rage.

A week later Philippa received a reply from Richard, telling her he was sorry she thought his actions so very bad, that he regretted them and that he would wait forever in the hope that she might change her mind. He also told her he had left money in his private cupboard for her to spend as she wished. She was to write him when it ran out and he would arrange with the goldsmith in Truro to release more.

His generosity almost dissolved her determination, but she brought up an image of her friends in their gaol, or hanging from a rope. She knew not which.

Knowing what he meant by his private cupboard, she made her way up the stairs. It was a sliding panel behind shelves in his bedchamber, the one he never used when they were together because he spent all his time in hers. That damned memory again!

She opened the panel to find a great deal of money in a small chest and a velvet purse. This was a total change from last time he left; then he had not wanted her comfort, had left her barely enough to feed herself. Had she not had the money still from the paintings he helped her to sell, she would have starved or depended on Alice who was still getting her pension from him.

Ladies in her position could not be seen to be trading in any way, so her paintings were sold privately to friends and friends of friends and where most men would have been horrified at their wives making money of their own, Richard was proud. That had warmed her heart at the time and still did when she remembered it.

As she took the purse and filled it to capacity with some of the coins, she still doubted that he could have betrayed her friends. But there seemed no other explanation and the fact of Selena being hidden away on his land bothered her a great deal. She had to help her; she was her friend and besides, she would not be in this position were it not for Lord Morton, but the knowledge that Selena was a wanted criminal and she was hiding her, gave her sleepless nights. While Selena stayed where she was, hidden in the hut, Madeleine was in danger. She had been wondering what she could do to remedy the situation, and now her heart sang with relief.

She hurried to the hut, being sure she was not followed, ready to give this loaded purse of coins to Selena, just so long as she would go away.

"There is enough there," she told her, "for you to get to Germany if you are careful."

The group had often spoken of escaping to Germany, the home of Martin Luther and where he was revered as a great teacher, not condemned as a heretic as he was here in England. Philippa, of course, had never considered going with them, as she always hoped to be reunited with her child, if not her husband.

Selena gave a satisfactory smile as she took the money.

"It is only right that he should pay for my journey, do you not think?" She remarked bitterly.

Philippa could not agree with her. This whole thing had destroyed all her hopes for the future, all her dreams of once more spending all her nights with the man she loved, and she did not feel like gloating or even thinking about how that had come to pass.

"Go," she said. "Wait until after dark, and stop for nothing. I wish you well."

Selena pulled her toward her and kissed her cheek.

"Thank you," she said. "I would have died were it not for you and I am sorry for you, that things have developed as they have. I can see you love him, despite that." She reached up a hand to Philippa's face, while she flinched away. "Perhaps you will forgive him in time. You deserve to be happy, but is he good enough for you?"

Her question made Philippa angry. Who was she to ask such a question, she who knew nothing about the wonderful years she had spent with her husband, before his brother ruined everything? She wanted Selena to go, she could not bear to be in her presence any longer.

"He is the best man in the world," she told her sorrowfully. "He made mistakes, but he is still the best man in the world."

Another letter arrived from him the following week, this one enclosing another letter and package for Madeleine and explaining in succinct and formal tones.

Philippa, this is the most suitable young man I have chosen to tentatively have contact with Madeleine with a view to marriage. I have made it clear that regular correspondence will be expected.

He is a viscount, the eldest son of the Earl, with good prospects. I have not read the letter myself, as I thought that something of an intrusion, but I am sure she will grant you permission to do so once she has read it for herself.

Please write me as to her reactions and thoughts. This is extremely important and I really wanted us to share the responsibility. If we have to do so by letter, so be it.

If there is anything I can do to change your mind, please, please tell me. Remember that I love you. Richard.

Those last three words at the end of such a formal letter unsettled her. She had to discover what was to become of her friends. If they should escape the death penalty and be released, or even serve a term of imprisonment, she might be able to convince herself that he had not realised the consequences of his actions. But it seemed unlikely that he did not know precisely what he was doing. He was the Lord of the Manor here and should always know what was happening, even if he was hundreds of miles away.

He may not have thought about what would happen to them, only that they would be locked away and unable to influence his wife, who he apparently did not trust. That hurt, just as it had all those years ago, even though it was a completely different situation.

Regular letters continued to come and Madeleine developed a mutual rapport with the young Viscount. Philippa thought it rather endearing and wondered if her own mother had felt the same when she was exchanging letters with her prospective bridegroom, who proved to be the man with whom she fell hopelessly in love and could not get out of her mind or her heart, no matter what he did to her.

CHAPTER ELEVEN

Philippa tried to make discreet enquiries as to the fate of her friends, but she could not risk a visit to the gaol itself. She knew very well there was only one person who could make those enquiries without arousing suspicion and she decided to swallow her pride and ask him. But it would have to wait until they met face to face, as anything in writing could be dangerous for all of them.

The young man to whom they intended to betroth their daughter was barely a month older than Madeleine, which meant that although she was of an age to wed at thirteen, he was not. That suited Philippa, as it seemed no time at all since Richard had brought her home and she had no wish to lose her again so soon.

Madeleine was getting a great deal of pleasure from her letters, both reading them and writing them, and the miniature he had sent showed him to be a handsome young man, with blonde hair and fine features.

Philippa went to her cabinet in her bedchamber and took from the top drawer the miniature which Richard had sent to her when they began their own pre-nuptial correspondence. She sat on the bed and looked at that handsome face, those dark eyes and shiny dark hair, and that little playful smile playing about his mouth. She smiled, remembering the day it had arrived at her father's house, remembering how excited she had been when she first saw it.

He looked much more mature now, of course; his beard had come through, but apart from that he had not changed much. He had filled out a little, but the main thing that had changed was the absence of that playful smile. Although he smiled, it was not the confident, comfortable smile of his youth, of their early years together, before the war with France, before Stephen.

A betrothal was arranged for Madeleine and Michael, to which both had consented eagerly and for which they would travel to London to attend an informal joining at Richard's London house. It would be an exchange of consent to marry, and although there was no priest in attendance, it would serve to seal the bargain and be legally binding. Madeleine was pleased she would meet her betrothed before the marriage.

Philippa could not decide if she would have liked to have met Richard before the marriage or not. As things turned out, there had been an immediate and intense attraction between them and she thought it might have been difficult to spend time apart once they had met. It would certainly have made no difference to their present situation.

The correspondence between Lord and Lady Morton regarding the betrothal had been painful. Each time she saw his handwriting her memory showed her his strong, naked shoulders, his lips on her breasts, his passionate kisses.

Each letter she wrote back was formal, concerning only the young couple, but she had to force herself to keep her own endearments to herself.

"How long will we have to stay in London?" Madeleine was asking now as her mother folded the latest letter from Richard. It outlined dates and arrangements for the betrothal ceremony and was couched in formal tones, but still ended with those three words *I love you.*

"A few days," Philippa replied. "A week at the most I should think. Your father has arranged a small gathering, just Michael and his sister and their parents, and us."

Madeleine gave a little thoughtful half smile then turned to her mother and reached out a hand to take hers.

"Do you think Father will come home with us?" She asked.

Philippa's heart leapt and it suddenly became real that in a few days she would see him again. What could she say? What answer could she give without lying?

"I doubt it, darling," she said at last. "He has a very important position at court and there is a lot of religious unrest. I am not sure the King can spare him."

"We cannot spare him either," Madeleine protested stubbornly. "The King can find another advisor; I cannot find another father."

Philippa put her arm around her and drew her close. Her innocent question had produced turmoil and ideas of Richard being here with them, all the time. She would love that to happen, but would it ever work after what he had done? Still, Madeleine had so little time left to be their child before she became someone's wife. She deserved to have both her parents with her for that final year, even if they parted with her marriage.

"Will Puddle come with us?"

"Oh, no, darling," Philippa replied. "I think Puddle will be happier staying where he is. It is such a long way and he is happy here. We can rely on the servants to look after him."

Madeleine nodded.

"You are right. It would be unfair to take him all that way, only to bring him all the way home again. What will happen to him when I marry, Mother? I have told Michael all about him, but he has not invited him to stay."

"Well, we will talk to Michael but I think he might be happier staying with me. It will be at least another year until you can marry and Puddle will be quite old in dog years by then. I would very much like to keep him here to look after me, for company, if you do not mind of course."

"You should have Father for company and to look after you," Madeleine remarked.

Philippa thought it best to change the subject. Madeleine was indeed growing up and speaking her mind. She knew there was more keeping her parents apart than she had been told and Philippa really did not want her to know all the details. She adored her father and she wanted nothing to spoil that.

The journey to London took three days. It might have been quicker were they prepared to suffer the discomfort without quite so many breaks, but they stopped for dinner at taverns on the way, and three times stopped at inns overnight.

Unlike Madeleine's journey to Cornwall with her father, they were able to share the bed, which was an adventure for Madeleine.

She had grown up in the year since her mother had looked up from the strange and friendly dog to be met with a vision from her dreams. That day will always be engraved in Philippa's mind; she really believed she was hallucinating and to know she was about to see Richard again had made her heart almost stop in her chest. She had been overjoyed and terrified at the same time when Madeleine told her he was there in the house.

Her first thought had been to find somewhere to hide, lest he still be angry, as the memory of his rage still frightened her. She expected him to treat her with disdain at the very least and while she listened to Madeleine's excited tales of their journey, of her life in London, her mind was busy deciding if she should try again to make him listen, to make him understand the truth.

She was convinced his life must be in some sort of danger for him to have brought their daughter to her. There could be no other explanation.

What she had not expected was a return to that passion, that closeness which they had always shared and when he finally left, having betrayed her friends to the church authorities, she wished they had kept their distance. It would have been much easier for her to dismiss him from her life, had she not been given the hope of a reconciliation.

They arrived at his London house at midday. He must have been watching for their arrival as he opened the door himself and stepped out into the courtyard before the carriage drew to a stop.

A servant came hurrying out behind him and opened the coach door, helped her down where she stood rigidly for a moment, wondering what to do, how to treat him.

Finally, she curtsied to him, as though they were strangers, when she really wanted to fling herself into his arms, to feel his heart beating against hers, to feel that special kiss which only he could give. He bowed formally.

"My Lady," he said.

"Father!"

Madeleine came tearing past her and did what her mother yearned to do, threw herself into his arms. He hugged her close, closed his eyes for a moment, then held her out before him in admiration.

"You look so grown up, so beautiful. I have missed you."

"I have missed you too, Father." Her eyes were huge as she looked up at him, then glanced at her mother.

"Madeleine is concerned," Philippa said, "that Michael will not like her."

"Of course he will like you," Richard assured her. "He will love you, how could he not? You have exchanged letters. You will meet him soon."

"Have you met him, Father?" She asked him hesitantly.

"I have. I would not have recommended him otherwise, would I? He is a very amiable young man and I believe what a lady might describe as handsome."

The girl's smile was infectious. Both her parents were smiling with her and she pulled away from him and ran into the house and up the stairs to the bedchamber she had not seen for over a year.

"Philippa," Richard said, turning towards her. "I expect you want to rest."

He offered his arm and they walked into the house, where he released her arm and made his way up the stairs, while she gathered up her skirts to follow him, wondering what sleeping arrangements he had organised for her. Her heart sank when he stepped into the chamber they had always shared many years ago, on the rare occasions she was in London, his own chamber. Her dismay was apparent.

"We have guests staying for the betrothal," he explained. "I do not want people wondering why we cannot share a bed. It would cause embarrassment for Madeleine." He paused and lifted her cloak from her shoulders. "At least not when I have no answer for them, because I do not know the answer myself."

She stared at him in astonishment. It could not possibly be true that he had no answer, it just could not.

"I will sleep on the trundle if you wish it," he said. "If I only knew what that final betrayal was you wrote about, I might be able to work my way through the puzzle."

"How can you say you do not know? After what you did?"

He stared at her angrily and she shuddered, suddenly recalling the day he had left her in a pool of blood. She drew herself up and closed her eyes, took a deep breath before opening them again to stare back at him. No, he was not that angry, not this time.

"What I did?" He replied. "I thought we were trying to move past that, trying to repair the damage, or at least patch it up."

"I am not talking about that!" She cried.

He sighed but no longer looked angry, for which she was relieved.

"What then? Was it so very bad to want to be sure those dangerous writings were out of my house? Was it really the last betrayal, after all the mistakes that had gone before?" He paused and his hands settled on her shoulders where he stood in front of her. She made no objection; she wanted to, but she had missed his touch so much she could not help but shiver. "Or were you having second thoughts and used that as an excuse to tell me to stay away? You needed no excuse, you should have known that. I told you that you only had to tell me to leave and I would. I did not need a reason; I needed only to know it was what you wanted."

She looked up at him, wondering why he was bringing that up again when it was quite obvious what she meant.

"But you wanted to accompany me only to discover who Selena was." He frowned and shook his head. "Can you deny it?"

"I do deny it, yes," he replied. "Why would I want to know about her? I only wanted to be sure that all the heretical works were away from my daughter. I do not understand what you are accusing me of."

"I am talking about my friends!" She shouted, then quickly lowered her voice. "How could you do that?"

"Your friends?"

"Yes, my friends who are languishing in prison or worse, since you betrayed them."

He stared at her with a frown, then shrugged and shook his head slowly.

"I am sorry, Philippa," he said, "but I have no idea what you are talking about."

He sounded genuine, but she knew better.

"Are you saying you are not the one who betrayed them?" She demanded. "You found my books, you made me return all my studies to Selena and even insisted on going with me so that you could discover who she was. Who else would it be?"

"You know I would never do that. How could you think I would do that?"

"How would I know what you are likely to do?"

He still seemed genuinely puzzled and for the first time she began to doubt her conviction that he had been the one. But who else?

"I cannot believe you thought me guilty of that," he said with a note of anger, which irritated her.

"Well now you know how it feels, at least," she said angrily.

He caught his breath.

"Why would I do that?" He asked with a sigh. "I had no reason to betray them."

"It was the only way you could be sure I would stay away from them, I suppose. You did not trust me to keep my word."

He sighed again and shook his head, then turned to the door and locked it while she wondered why he had done that. There was only one reason he had ever locked the door and she was angry again that he would take it for granted after all this time. Still, it was up to him; he had the right and she could not stop him, even if she tried. He was much stronger than she, but he would not do that would he? He was not his brother.

"Why have you locked the door?" She asked.

"To prevent Madeleine interrupting us, that is all. Nothing sinister. It is important that we have this talk uninterrupted."

He took her shoulders in his strong, warm hands and held her so he could look into her eyes.

"Have we wasted yet another year because of a misunderstanding?" He said. "I did not betray your friends. They were no threat to me so why should I? In fact, if any one of them had thought it they could easily have informed on you and you would have been there with them, leaving Madeleine alone and without either her father or her mother. Is it likely I would have done that?"

She suppressed a sob, wondering if she had made the mistake this time, hoping she had and he was really telling the truth.

"If not you, then who?" She demanded. "No one else knew about us."

"Someone did, obviously." He still kept his grip on her shoulders, still gazed at her, then he asked in a grave voice: "Do you believe me?"

"I want to," she answered. "You cannot know how much I want to."

He looked at her for a few more minutes, his eyes searching her face.

"I swear to you, Philippa, it was not me. I had nothing to gain and I would never have done that. It was not distrust of you that made me insist on going with you; it was a need to be sure that Madeleine never saw those books, for her own sake and for yours. It was foolish, I know, but I had not seen you for a long time and it was a shock to learn you were studying Luther at all." He took her chin gently in his hand and tilted her face up to look at him. "Please say you believe me."

"I would love to believe you," she said. "But there is no other explanation. There was a time I would have wagered everything on it not being you, when I could have said you would never do such a thing, but you did a lot of things I never thought you capable of, that I still look back on with disbelief."

"I too look back on that time with disbelief," he said softly. "I cannot believe what I did, how I behaved, and I cannot believe that I destroyed a good marriage and a beautiful love. But I did and I would not have betrayed your friends for that very reason, because I was hoping for another chance and I would have done nothing to interfere with that. But you do not believe me and I cannot blame you for that." He took both her hands in his and his eyes met hers before he went on. "I have something to tell you."

"What?" She asked.

She was nervous now, thinking that perhaps he had tired of this long distance relationship and wanted grounds to dissolve the marriage after all. She could not bear that idea, no matter what she believed about him.

"I have resigned my post at court," he replied. "After the betrothal I shall be returning to Cornwall with you and Madeleine, whether you want me there or not."

She made no reply, but her heart jolted with anticipation at the idea of his being with her, while she still could not forgive his betrayal. Given such close proximity, she knew she would not be able to resist him. She was once more torn in two directions and she hated it.

"The house is big enough." he went on. "We need see nothing of each other if that is your wish."

"It is still your house, My Lord," she murmured.

"It is indeed, but I promised it to you for your sanctuary. Now I have changed my mind."

"Why? You are not one to break your promises."

"I have several reasons, one of which is the danger of being too close to the King at this time. He turned the country upside down to marry this woman and she has still not produced a healthy son. He is as volatile as a wild dog and one never knows how he is likely to turn. He asks questions, opinions but he may want a different one to the one he wanted yesterday. I cannot live like that and I believe it to be too dangerous, certainly not worth staying for, especially when all I ever wanted was to live quietly with my family."

His description of life at court made her nervous and she would have asked, nay begged him to come home for his own safety, had he not decided anyway.

"What else?" She asked.

"I am tired of this long distance marriage of ours. I decided long ago that I want to try to make amends, before I knew what it was you suspected me of. I see that to do that I will need to go home and find the real culprit." He paused and smiled softly. "Then there is Madeleine. This is the last year she will be with us and I do not want to miss out on that. We should all be together, for her sake."

"I agree, of course. Neither one of us should miss out on that." She frowned thoughtfully. "How will you find the real culprit? How will you prove me wrong?"

"I have some influence," he said with a smile. "I know I am not guilty, so it follows that someone must be. Are you anywhere near believing me yet?"

"Yes. And I do want you home, more than anything."

"Can I kiss you now then?" He asked and she was relieved to see that playful smile once more. If there was one thing she longed to see all those years ago, before they met to be married, it was that playful smile which the clever artist had worked into his portrait.

"Yes, please," she replied.

He needed no further encouragement. His lips came down on hers and he kissed her with that special kiss which sent thrills travelling through her body. Her arms went around his waist as she kissed him back and she pulled his shirt out of his waistband and unfastened his breeches. He unlaced her bodice and removed it, then untied her petticoats, letting them fall to the floor while his fingers found the ribbon ties of her shift. His hands moved down her neck and slipped the silk fabric from her shoulders, releasing her breasts to be crushed against his chest as he held her tightly against him.

He lifted her off her feet and placed her on the bed, then climbed up beside her, his hands gently stroking her breasts, her stomach, inside her thighs while her fingers flirted with the hair on his chest.

Their breathing became louder and faster and she hoped nobody was listening. She suddenly thought of Madeleine and realised this was why he locked the door, this was what he hoped for all along, but he would never force her; that was not his way nor ever would be.

The feel of him inside her made her cry out with joy as he moved, gently at first, then gradually becoming faster and stronger. Oh, God! Why had she wasted so much time?

Madeleine waited outside the door, a little smile on her face when she turned the knob and discovered it locked.

CHAPTER TWELVE

The betrothal was held in the ballroom of the London house, which had been strewn with flowers. It was a simple exchange of consent, a promise from both of them to marry, and Madeleine had asked Richard to tie their hands together with a scarf as they had done in olden times.

Madeleine wore a pale blue satin gown covered with cloth of silver and a cloth of silver veil covered her long, chestnut hair. Her headdress was the same blue satin with tiny diamonds sparkling like stars all over.

She was very excited that morning and very nervous, although there were no formal vows to make and only close family to watch.

"Oh, my darling," Philippa said when she came down the stairs. "You look so beautiful." She turned to her husband and smiled. "Richard?"

"You certainly do."

He gave his arm to his daughter on one side and his wife on the other. Philippa wore satin too, which was not her accustomed choice of fabric as she felt it too stiff and formal, but today was for Madeleine and sacrifices needed to be made. Her gown was crimson with embroidered sleeves and a square, low cut neckline. Her headdress clipped onto her face in front of her ears to cover the scar completely.

The couple smiled nervously at each other, Madeleine held Michael's right hand with her own and her father tied the scarf loosely around their wrists.

Goblets of wine were exchanged, and they kissed. As her parents watched, the couple kissed a second time, impetuously, and this kiss was longer. Philippa smiled happily, knowing her husband had chosen well. This young man was already half in love with her daughter.

"I hope they will find the love that we found," she said, holding his hand as they watched.

"I hope so too," he replied. "And I hope that we too can find it again."

Philippa was still torn in two. After her week in London, where she willingly and happily spent each night in Richard's bed, she would have been happier than she had in years were in not for this question which hung over them.

Madeleine was as happy as that first day when she had played in the waves with her dog, so pleased to be back home again. But things had changed since then, she had grown up a lot and talked constantly of Michael and the things he had told her, how he had promised her a puppy once they were married. He had given her a beautiful sapphire ring which reflected the silver cloth on her gown and which she stared at periodically all the way home in the carriage.

She also stared at her father where he sat across from her and her mother, as though she was not sure he was real. When told that he would be returning with them, her face had broken into a smile of sheer delight.

"Really?" She had asked. "He is coming home to stay? Really?"

Philippa reached out and took her hand.

"Really. We have decided that life is too short to waste on misunderstandings. We love each other and we are miserable apart. They are reasons enough to be together again."

They managed to make good time and completed the journey with only one overnight stop at an inn where they shared a bed, while Madeleine slept on the trundle and hoped there were no rats. They were all exhausted by the time they reached home but that did not stop Madeleine from running into the house excitedly, calling out for her dog.

Puddle was so excited to see them, his tail was wagging so fast it almost tipped him over and he licked them all in his delight. They watched him follow Madeleine outside and on to the beach.

"Oh, Richard!" Philippa said, turning to him as she tossed her cloak aside. "I am so very happy to have you home. I believe you, really I do. You have nothing to prove to me."

"Oh, but I do. I have to prove it to myself as well."

He gathered her into his arms and kissed her, holding her close against him, pressing his body to hers so that she felt the stirring of his desire.

"We will have to wait until bed time," she whispered seductively.

"Does this mean I can share your part of the house?" He said mischievously. "We are not going to avoid each other after all?"

She reached up and kissed him again and turned as she heard a step behind her. Alice stood on the bottom stair, a puzzled frown on her face.

"Alice," Richard turned to her with a bow.

"My Lord," she replied and he noted with relief the absence of that contempt in her eyes. She may not be ready yet to use his given name, but at least she seemed to have abandoned her hatred.

"I shall go," he said. "I want to make some enquiries in the village before it gets too late. I shall not rest until I am sure you know the truth."

Philippa watched him go then turned back to the old nurse with a smile of delight.

"My Lady?" She said. "I was not expecting His Lordship home."

"Neither was I," she said, "but I was wrong this time. It was not him who betrayed my friends and he is going to find out who it really was."

Alice continued on her way down the stairs and took Philippa into her arms.

"You look so happy," she said as she hugged her, "happier than I have seen you in years."

Philippa smiled at the old nurse. There was one thing she wanted now to make her future hopes complete.

"You will forgive him?" She asked.

"To see you this happy," Alice replied, "I would forgive the devil himself."

The following day, Richard set out to visit the magistrate in Truro. It seemed that apart from Selena and her father, Philippa had only known them by their given names. They had all thought it safer that way and they were likely right. He learned names from the villagers, and he had also learned it was only Master Wright who had been arrested and imprisoned, no one else. That was not what Philippa believed and he was puzzled.

He wanted to know why, as it seemed unlikely to him, but more than that he wanted to know who had informed on him since he knew it was not him.

He opened the door without knocking and stood in the doorway watching the magistrate as he looked up from his table and arched his eyebrows.

"My Lord," he said, getting quickly to his feet. "I had no idea you were back."

No, Richard thought, no one knew he had been back before did they? His business then had been solely with his wife and daughter and he had done nothing to reveal his presence to anyone else. As far as the magistrate knew, he had been away for eight years.

"Sit, Sir," he said. "I came to enquire about a prisoner I believe you have serving a sentence in Truro, one Master Wright."

The magistrate looked frightened for a moment, then he went back to his chair and sat down.

"I know the man, My Lord," he replied hesitantly. "I believe some agreement was made with the Bishop that he was to escape execution. It was not my doing, My Lord."

"Agreement?" Richard asked. "Was there no trial?"

"There was, My Lord, but it was conducted under canon law and presided over by the Bishop."

"Of course," Richard soothed him. "It was a church matter, I see that. Something I would have expected the Bishop to have an interest in. But I think you can answer my questions, just the same."

The magistrate's eyes moved nervously around the room as though afraid the Bishop might be listening.

"What are you afraid of?" Lord Morton asked.

"Nothing, My Lord." Richard raised an eyebrow. "Very well," the magistrate went on. "I was told at the time to tell no one. But I cannot imagine that included you, My Lord."

"So tell me. Tell me about the agreement and who made it. Tell me why a prison sentence was given by the church to a heretic they would more likely have condemned to death."

"The agreement was made by the informant, My Lord," the magistrate replied quickly, as though he wanted to get the words out before he changed his mind. "She was promised he would not be executed. She had valuable information, so His Grace went along with it."

"She?"

"Yes, My Lord. The lady in question was very brave, considering the condemned man was her father."

As Richard stared at him he could feel the anger begin to gather inside him.

"Selena Wright?" He asked incredulously. "It was his daughter, Selena who betrayed him? And it was only him, no one else?"

"Yes, My Lord. I am surprised that you know the woman."

He had to stop himself from voicing his thoughts. She was the one who told his wife it had to be him who betrayed them, told her it was the whole group, convinced her to ask him to stay in London, when all the time she had been the traitor. He could only assume she was one of those spiteful people who could not bear to see anyone happy. And Philippa thought she was her friend.

"Yes," he said. "I know her."

He felt his fists clenching, then noticed the magistrate's eyes were growing round with fear.

"What a pity you do not have her here," Richard went on. "I would almost be glad to light the faggots myself."

"Forgive me, My Lord. I had no idea and neither did the Bishop, I am sure. We thought she was a good Catholic trying to do the right thing."

"How much longer is his sentence?"

"Indefinite, My Lord."

"That must change. I want him released as soon as possible and anyone else in the group."

"No one else, My Lord."

No one else. Here his wife had been blaming him and thinking she was herself inadvertently the cause of the deaths of all of them, when all the time it was only him and at the behest of his own daughter. Richard had to know why.

"I will visit the Bishop myself today about Master Wright's release," Richard said. "But I want to see him first."

.

Philippa sat on the balcony, watching the waves and Madeleine where she sat on a rock and read her latest letter from Michael. A small, contented smile played about her mouth as she read and Philippa felt a little glow of contentment herself. She recalled sitting in her father's garden all those years ago, feeling the cool mist from the fountain, the same little smile on her own face as she read one of her letters from Richard. Madeleine had told her father it seemed they had fallen in love through those letters and she was right. She determined to read them again, all of them, and she wanted him to be with her when she did. She wondered if they could recapture those same naive thoughts and feelings they both had then, when all they longed to do was meet and talk and kiss, perhaps hold each other. Neither of them had any idea of the bliss which would follow those simple gestures.

She sighed softly. She had missed out on her daughter's childhood, she had been wrongly blamed and punished for something that was no fault of her own, but that time seemed to be already fading into the distant past. She would not have Madeleine for long, but she had her now and she had the love of her life back with her, loving her as he always had. She hoped Stephen was watching them from whatever hell he had been condemned to, she hoped he was being penalised for his sin, for the pain he caused to the one person to whom he should have shown loyalty, his own brother.

She had been so deep in thought, she did not hear his step behind her, only felt his lips on her neck and his hands on her shoulders. She looked up and smiled and he bent his head and kissed her longingly.

"Well?" She asked. "Did you learn anything?"

"I did," he answered. "You are not going to like it."

"Who?"

"Selena."

She sat up straight; his words shocked her and she thought he must have got it wrong.

"No. There must be some mistake. Why would she? She was more zealous than any of us, so much so that she went to Germany."

She suddenly remembered where Selena got the money to pay her passage to Germany and she stopped talking, hoping he did not ask. She did not want him to know he had paid for it.

"It had nothing to do with religion," he said. "Her father had arranged a marriage for her with a man almost three times her age and with two grown up children. He was trying to force her into it, insisting that if she did not marry this man he would throw her out to starve on the streets."

"How do you know this?"

"He told me. I went to the prison to see him, and to tell him I would persuade the Bishop to agree to his release. He always believed that to be her reason, and it seems plausible to me."

"But why did she have to blame you?" Philippa demanded. "Why did she have to convince me no one else could have betrayed us?"

He moved around to sit beside her, then put his arm around her and kissed her cheek.

"That was only part of it," he told her. "None of the others were caught, as she told you; only her father. She wanted you to have more for which to blame me."

Philippa was silent for a few moments, trying to take in this new information.

"That was a spiteful thing to do," she murmured at last, "just when I was thinking we might have a chance."

"I think that might have been her reason," he said.

"Why? She was supposed to be my friend. Do you think she wanted me to be unhappy?"

"I think she was jealous," he went on. "She was being forced into a marriage with a man who was very unattractive to a young girl, for no better reason it seems than that he owned the fishmongery and was a dedicated Lutheran. Then she meets me, sees we are contemplating a reconciliation and decides she will have her father imprisoned so he cannot force her into the marriage and ease her jealousy all in one go."

"I cannot believe it."

"It is supposition," he answered. "But without flattering myself too much, I do believe I am a more attractive prospect than an old man who is overweight and stinks of fish."

He showed her that playful little smile again, the one he always wore before their separation, before Stephen and she leaned over and kissed his lips.

"He reminded me of Stephen," Richard remarked.

"The fishmonger?"

"No. Master Wright. He knew why his daughter had betrayed him, condemned him to years of hard labour, but he was not sorry; he was only sorry he ended up in gaol. If he had it to do again, he would do no different. It was as though he thought she had no right to question him, and still felt the same. He seemed angrier that she had escaped the marriage and moved beyond his control than he did that she had informed on him. Stephen had that same attitude when he finally confessed to me what he had done; he was not sorry for what he had done, only that he might go to Hell."

"Master Wright always was a bit like that," she answered. "When we had our meetings, he treated all the women as though they would not understand without his guidance. He would have been happier had there been no women included and I almost gave myself away on several occasions just to shut him up, to get the better of him."

"Gave yourself away?" He said. "I do not understand."

She turned to look at his puzzled frown and realised she had told him nothing about her meetings with the protestants. He had not asked and she had been so angry at his attitude, she had not bothered to enlighten him.

"None of them knew who I was," she said, "not until that last day, when I returned the books to Selena and she met you. Did you not notice the look of surprise on her face. That may be why she tried to blame you; she seemed annoyed that I had told her nothing about my husband and daughter. I could have been in charge of that group; I could even have ordered Master Wright to abandon the idea of the marriage, if only I had known. I wonder why she did not ask for my help once she did know."

"It was likely because of me. I doubt she imagined I would allow it if she was used to a man behaving like him. Why did you not reveal yourself?"

"I had no right to involve you in an illegal activity," she answered. "Had they known who I was, they might have believed I had your support. I would never have done that."

His eyes met hers and he felt ashamed all over again for suspecting her all those years ago, and for not trusting her with those books. She had kept his name out of it, all those years meeting with these people, she had never once let them know who she was, even though it would have been to her advantage. She protected him; where the hell was he when she needed him to protect her?

"Madeleine seems happy," Richard said. He still sat on the balcony, his arm around his wife, watching his daughter as she threw the ball into the sea for her dog. She still clutched her latest letter from Michael in her hand and every few minutes she would stop and reread it, that same little smile on her pretty mouth each time she did so.

"She is," Philippa replied. "You chose well."

"I think I did," he replied. "I certainly tried. I can only hope he is not as careless with her love as I was with yours."

She leaned over and kissed him, a long, tender kiss and her arms wrapped themselves around his waist and held him tight.

"You know," she said, "we will never be able to move on if we dwell. It still churns me up inside to think of, so it is best not to think of it at all."

"What do you want to do?"

She smiled and her eyes met his.

"I want to go and find those letters we wrote to each other before our marriage, I want to see if we can recapture that innocence we had then, that trust. We can never have the exclusiveness we once did, but we can pretend and it will begin with our letters."

"I would like that," he said. "Madeleine says they are very fond letters, that we must have fallen in love through those letters. Perhaps we can do that again. Anything else?"

"Yes. When we have read the letters, we will pretend some more. We will pretend it is our wedding night again, that we are sharing our bodies for the very first time. We will be shy and nervous and excited, we will pretend it is all new and enchanting."

His warm smile touched her heart. She could see she had pleased him with her fantasy.

"I would like that," he said. "We can never recapture what we lost, we can never go back in time, but..."

"We can pretend."

THE END

Newgate Prison was a prison in London, at the corner of Newgate Street and Old Bailey just inside the City of London. It was originally located at the site of a gate in the Roman London Wall. The gate/prison was rebuilt in the 12th century, and demolished in 1777. The prison was extended and rebuilt many times, and remained in use for over 700 years, from 1188 to 1902.

The first prison at Newgate was built in 1188 on the orders of Henry II. It was significantly enlarged in 1236, and the executors of Lord Mayor Richard Whittington were granted a license to renovate the prison in 1422. The prison was destroyed in the Great Fire of London in 1666, and was rebuilt in 1672, extending into new buildings on the south side of the street.

Author's Note: Thank you for reading The Wronged Wife. If you have enjoyed it please consider my other books:

The Romany Princess

Mirielle
The Judas Pledge
The Flawed Mistress
The Scent of Roses
To Catch A Demon
The Viscount's Birthright
The Adulteress
A Man in Mourning

The first chapter of each of these books can be read on my blog at http://historical-fiction-on-kindle.blogspot.co.uk

Printed in Great Britain
by Amazon.co.uk, Ltd.,
Marston Gate.